THE PELICAN SHAKESPEARE

GENERAL EDITOR ALFRED HARBAGE

CYMBELINE

WILLIAM SHAKESPEARE

CYMBELINE

EDITED BY ROBERT B. HEILMAN

PENGUIN BOOKS

PENGUIN BOOKS
Published by the Penguin Group
Penguin Books USA Inc.,
375 Hudson Street, New York, New York 10014, U.S.A.
Penguin Books Ltd, 27 Wrights Lane, London W8 5TZ, England
Penguin Books Australia Ltd, Ringwood, Victoria, Australia
Penguin Books Canada Ltd, 10 Alcorn Avenue
Toronto, Ontario, Canada M4V 3B2
Penguin Books (N.Z.) Ltd, 182–190 Wairau Road, Auckland 10, New Zealand

Penguin Books Ltd, Registered Offices:
Harmondsworth, Middlesex, England

First published in *The Pelican Shakespeare* 1964
This revised edition first published 1979

8   10   9

Library of Congress catalog card number: 77-98378
ISBN 0 14 0714.28 6

Printed in the United States of America
Set in Monotype Ehrhardt

CONTENTS

PUBLISHER'S NOTE

Soon after the thirty-eight volumes forming *The Pelican Shakespeare* had been published, they were brought together in *The Complete Pelican Shakespeare*. The editorial revisions and new textual features are explained in detail in the General Editor's Preface to the one-volume edition. They have all been incorporated in the present volume. The following should be mentioned in particular:

The lines are not numbered in arbitrary units. Instead all lines are numbered which contain a word, phrase, or allusion explained in the glossarial notes. In the occasional instances where there is a long stretch of unannotated text, certain lines are numbered in italics to serve the conventional reference purpose.

The intrusive and often inaccurate place-headings inserted by early editors are omitted (as is becoming standard practise), but for the convenience of those who miss them, an indication of locale now appears as first item in the annotation of each scene.

In the interest of both elegance and utility, each speech-prefix is set in a separate line when the speaker's lines are in verse, except when these words form the second half of a pentameter line. Thus the verse form of the speech is kept visually intact, and turned-over lines are avoided. What is printed as verse and what is printed as prose has, in general, the authority of the original texts. Departures from the original texts in this regard have only the authority of editorial tradition and the judgment of the Pelican editors; and, in a few instances, are admittedly arbitrary.

SHAKESPEARE AND
HIS STAGE

William Shakespeare was christened in Holy Trinity Church, Stratford-upon-Avon, April 26, 1564. His birth is traditionally assigned to April 23. He was the eldest of four boys and two girls who survived infancy in the family of John Shakespeare, glover and trader of Henley Street, and his wife Mary Arden, daughter of a small landowner of Wilmcote. In 1568 John was elected Bailiff (equivalent to Mayor) of Stratford, having already filled the minor municipal offices. The town maintained for the sons of the burgesses a free school, taught by a university graduate and offering preparation in Latin sufficient for university entrance; its early registers are lost, but there can be little doubt that Shakespeare received the formal part of his education in this school.

On November 27, 1582, a license was issued for the marriage of William Shakespeare (aged eighteen) and Ann Hathaway (aged twenty-six), and on May 26, 1583, their child Susanna was christened in Holy Trinity Church. The inference that the marriage was forced upon the youth is natural but not inevitable; betrothal was legally binding at the time, and was sometimes regarded as conferring conjugal rights. Two additional children of the marriage, the twins Hamnet and Judith, were christened on February 2, 1585. Meanwhile the prosperity of the elder Shakespeares had declined, and William was impelled to seek a career outside Stratford.

The tradition that he spent some time as a country

7

teacher is old but unverifiable. Because of the absence of records his early twenties are called the "lost years," and only one thing about them is certain – that at least some of these years were spent in winning a place in the acting profession. He may have begun as a provincial trouper, but by 1592 he was established in London and prominent enough to be attacked. In a pamphlet of that year, *Groats-worth of Wit*, the ailing Robert Greene complained of the neglect which university writers like himself had suffered from actors, one of whom was daring to set up as a playwright:

... an vpstart Crow, beautified with our feathers, that with his *Tygers hart wrapt in a Players hyde*, supposes he is as well able to bombast out a blanke verse as the best of you: and beeing an absolute *Iohannes fac totum*, is in his owne conceit the onely Shake-scene in a countrey.

The pun on his name, and the parody of his line "O tiger's heart wrapped in a woman's hide" (*3 Henry VI*), pointed clearly to Shakespeare. Some of his admirers protested, and Henry Chettle, the editor of Greene's pamphlet, saw fit to apologize:

... I am as sory as if the originall fault had beene my fault, because my selfe haue seene his demeanor no lesse ciuill than he excelent in the qualitie he professes: Besides, diuers of worship haue reported his vprightnes of dealing, which argues his honesty, and his facetious grace in writting, that approoues his Art. (Prefatory epistle, *Kind-Harts Dreame*)

The plague closed the London theatres for many months in 1592–94, denying the actors their livelihood. To this period belong Shakespeare's two narrative poems, *Venus and Adonis* and *The Rape of Lucrece*, both dedicated to the Earl of Southampton. No doubt the poet was rewarded with a gift of money as usual in such cases, but he did no further dedicating and we have no reliable information on whether Southampton, or anyone else, became his regular patron. His sonnets, first mentioned in 1598 and published without his consent in 1609, are intimate without being

8

explicitly autobiographical. They seem to commemorate the poet's friendship with an idealized youth, rivalry with a more favored poet, and love affair with a dark mistress; and his bitterness when the mistress betrays him in conjunction with the friend; but it is difficult to decide precisely what the "story" is, impossible to decide whether it is fictional or true. The true distinction of the sonnets, at least of those not purely conventional, rests in the universality of the thoughts and moods they express, and in their poignancy and beauty.

In 1594 was formed the theatrical company known until 1603 as the Lord Chamberlain's men, thereafter as the King's men. Its original membership included, besides Shakespeare, the beloved clown Will Kempe and the famous actor Richard Burbage. The company acted in various London theatres and even toured the provinces, but it is chiefly associated in our minds with the Globe Theatre built on the south bank of the Thames in 1599. Shakespeare was an actor and joint owner of this company (and its Globe) through the remainder of his creative years. His plays, written at the average rate of two a year, together with Burbage's acting won it its place of leadership among the London companies.

Individual plays began to appear in print, in editions both honest and piratical, and the publishers became increasingly aware of the value of Shakespeare's name on the title pages. As early as 1598 he was hailed as the leading English dramatist in the *Palladis Tamia* of Francis Meres:

As *Plautus* and *Seneca* are accounted the best for Comedy and Tragedy among the Latines, so *Shakespeare* among the English is the most excellent in both kinds for the stage: for Comedy, witnes his *Gentlemen of Verona*, his *Errors*, his *Loue labors lost*, his *Loue labours wonne* [at one time in print but no longer extant, at least under this title], his *Midsummers night dream*, & his *Merchant of Venice*; for Tragedy, his *Richard the 2*, *Richard the 3*, *Henry the 4*, *King Iohn*, *Titus Andronicus*, and his *Romeo and Iuliet*.

9

The note is valuable both in indicating Shakespeare's prestige and in helping us to establish a chronology. In the second half of his writing career, history plays gave place to the great tragedies; and farces and light comedies gave place to the problem plays and symbolic romances. In 1623, seven years after his death, his former fellow-actors, John Heminge and Henry Condell, cooperated with a group of London printers in bringing out his plays in collected form. The volume is generally known as the First Folio.

Shakespeare had never severed his relations with Stratford. His wife and children may sometimes have shared his London lodgings, but their home was Stratford. His son Hamnet was buried there in 1596, and his daughters Susanna and Judith were married there in 1607 and 1616 respectively. (His father, for whom he had secured a coat of arms and thus the privilege of writing himself gentleman, died in 1601, his mother in 1608.) His considerable earnings in London, as actor-sharer, part owner of the Globe, and playwright, were invested chiefly in Stratford property. In 1597 he purchased for £60 New Place, one of the two most imposing residences in the town. A number of other business transactions, as well as minor episodes in his career, have left documentary records. By 1611 he was in a position to retire, and he seems gradually to have withdrawn from theatrical activity in order to live in Stratford. In March, 1616, he made a will, leaving token bequests to Burbage, Heminge, and Condell, but the bulk of his estate to his family. The most famous feature of the will, the bequest of the second-best bed to his wife, reveals nothing about Shakespeare's marriage; the quaintness of the provision seems commonplace to those familiar with ancient testaments. Shakespeare died April 23, 1616, and was buried in the Stratford church where he had been christened. Within seven years a monument was erected to his memory on the north wall of the chancel. Its portrait bust and the Droeshout engraving on the title page of the First Folio provide the only likenesses with an established claim to authenticity. The best verbal vignette was written by his rival Ben Jonson, the more impressive for being imbedded in a context mainly critical:

... I loved the man, and doe honour his memory (on this side idolatry) as much as any. Hee was indeed honest, and of an open and free nature: had an excellent Phantsie, brave notions, and gentle expressions. ... (*Timber or Discoveries*, ca. 1623–30)

*

The reader of Shakespeare's plays is aided by a general knowledge of the way in which they were staged. The King's men acquired a roofed and artificially lighted theatre only toward the close of Shakespeare's career, and then only for winter use. Nearly all his plays were designed for performance in such structures as the Globe – a three-tiered amphitheatre with a large rectangular platform extending to the center of its yard. The plays were staged by daylight, by large casts brilliantly costumed, but with only a minimum of properties, without scenery, and quite possibly without intermissions. There was a rear stage gallery for action "above," and a curtained rear recess for "discoveries" and other special effects, but by far the major portion of any play was enacted upon the projecting platform, with episode following episode in swift succession, and with shifts of time and place signaled the audience only by the momentary clearing of the stage between the episodes. Information about the identity of the characters and, when necessary, about the time and place of the action was incorporated in the dialogue. No place-headings have been inserted in the present editions; these are apt to obscure the original fluidity of structure, with the emphasis upon action and speech rather than scenic background. (Indications of place are supplied in the footnotes.) The acting, including that of the youthful apprentices to the profession who performed the parts of women, was highly skillful, with a premium placed upon grace of gesture and beauty of diction. The audiences, a cross section of the general public, commonly numbered a thousand, sometimes more than two thousand. Judged by the type of plays they applauded, these audiences were not only large but also perceptive.

THE TEXTS OF THE PLAYS

About half of Shakespeare's plays appeared in print for the first time in the folio volume of 1623. The others had been published individually, usually in quarto volumes, during his lifetime or in the six years following his death. The copy used by the printers of the quartos varied greatly in merit, sometimes representing Shakespeare's true text, sometimes only a debased version of that text. The copy used by the printers of the folio also varied in merit, but was chosen with care. Since it consisted of the best available manuscripts, or the more acceptable quartos (although frequently in editions other than the first), or of quartos corrected by reference to manuscripts, we have good or reasonably good texts of most of the thirty-seven plays.

In the present series, the plays have been newly edited from quarto or folio texts, depending, when a choice offered, upon which is now regarded by bibliographical specialists as the more authoritative. The ideal has been to reproduce the chosen texts with as few alterations as possible, beyond occasional relineation, expansion of abbreviations, and modernization of punctuation and spelling. Emendation is held to a minimum, and such material as has been added, in the way of stage directions and lines supplied by an alternative text, has been enclosed in square brackets.

None of the plays printed in Shakespeare's lifetime were divided into acts and scenes, and the inference is that the author's own manuscripts were not so divided. In the folio collection, some of the plays remained undivided, some were divided into acts, and some were divided into acts and scenes. During the eighteenth century all of the plays were divided into acts and scenes, and in the Cambridge edition of the mid-nineteenth century, from which the influential Globe text derived, this division was more or less regularized and the lines were numbered. Many useful works of reference employ the act–scene–line apparatus thus established.

Since this act–scene division is obviously convenient, but is of very dubious authority so far as Shakespeare's own structural principles are concerned, or the original manner of staging his plays, a problem is presented to modern editors. In the present series the act–scene division is retained marginally, and may be viewed as a reference aid like the line numbering. A star marks the points of division when these points have been determined by a cleared stage indicating a shift of time and place in the action of the play, or when no harm results from the editorial assumption that there is such a shift. However, at those points where the established division is clearly misleading – that is, where continuous action has been split up into separate "scenes" – the star is omitted and the distortion corrected. This mechanical expedient seemed the best means of combining utility and accuracy.

THE GENERAL EDITOR

INTRODUCTION

In *Romeo and Juliet* (ca. 1595) Romeo, believing that Juliet is dead, enters her tomb, takes poison there, and dies. Upon awaking and finding Romeo dead, Juliet stabs herself and dies. In *Antony and Cleopatra* (ca. 1607) Antony, believing that Cleopatra is dead, falls on his sword and thus brings about his death. In consequence, Cleopatra resolves on death by the poisonous bite of the asp. Compare these roughly similar situations with certain events in *Cymbeline* (ca. 1609–10). Imogen, recovering like Juliet from a drug which has brought about her apparent death, opens her eyes upon a corpse which she believes to be her husband's. But, though she faints, she neither takes her life nor thinks of doing so. When Posthumus receives apparent evidence of Imogen's death, he too goes on living, though he has the added burden of remorse; true, he thinks of death, but only as a natural hazard of the war that he chooses to enter.

To be sure, different lovers have different personalities. But behind the variations of personality lie literary factors that influence the strikingly different outcomes of situations up to a point strikingly alike. Different conventions are at work: in *Romeo* and *Antony*, those of tragedy; in *Cymbeline*, those of dramatic romance. As it is used here, *convention* does not mean a formula, stereotype, or constricting rule, but rather a certain point of view, a way of perceiving human behavior, of understanding it and responding to it emotionally. A convention is a bond, though a flexible one, between playwright and audience; it involves a loose, unspoken agreement about attitude and procedure; it is rooted in shared expectations, though these may be unarticulated, general rather than specific, and open to great imaginative transformation by the artist. The tragic convention interprets life as a clash between, on the one hand, transcendent principles of order and, on the other, urgencies of desire and intensities of feeling that, once they are in play, lead inevitably to destructive encounters and somber catastrophes. The convention of romance approaches life in terms of the ultimate reconcilability of desires and circumstances; though ambitions and needs may be great, they tend to fall within a realm of moral possibility; and circumstances, though they may be antagonistic for a long period, eventually yield to meritorious humanity. The tragic involvement is total, reckless, irremediable; the protagonist is wholly committed to a situation which seems to enfold all of life's possibilities. In contrast, in the convention represented in *Cymbeline* the personal impulse does not become identical with, or aspire to dominate, all of reality; beyond the individuals there is an independent life that makes legitimate claims or offers alternative possibilities. For Imogen and for Posthumus, the loved one does not become the only way, a *sine qua non;* Imogen, though grief-stricken, can cling to life, and Posthumus can fight for his country. Thus both survive for an unravelling of circumstance that offers them, in the end, satisfactions unforeseen at the moment of apparent disaster. (In the matter of circumstances romance may be contrasted with two later conventions that reacted against it: whereas romance treats circumstances as being ultimately malleable or beneficent, realism regards them as independent and subject to their own laws, and naturalism treats them as either indifferent or positively hostile to human endeavor.)

In both tragedy and romance human beings are reservoirs of strong passions. Yet romance has a greater sense of limits – of the decorum or principle or rational endowment or even pragmatic awareness that balances off the passion and holds it back from the irretrievable. Tragedy is more attuned to extremes and depths, to profound conflicts within personality (as in Macbeth, Othello, and Lear). Cymbeline, caught between the Roman Empire and British loyalty, between wife and daughter, between his dynastic plans and Imogen's emotions, is potentially a tragic figure; but Shakespeare does not portray him as destroyed by irreconcilable forces. Romance either does not see the painful inner conflict or treats it as reparable this side of catastrophe; for the clash of impulses it will most often substitute the clash of persons – sometimes simply of the good ones who come out all right in the end and the bad ones who go down. Cymbeline's Queen is all unscrupulousness; she has none of Lady Macbeth's capacity for destructive inner stresses. Cloten is self-seeking and vengeful, but as a character in romance he is not credited with the brains or drive to do permanent damage. Again, the Cymbeline–Imogen relationship has interesting resemblances to the Capulet–Juliet and the Lear–Cordelia relationships. Capulet and Cymbeline both want to impose unwelcome marriages on their daughters: in the tragedy, the father is relentless and hence contributes to the daughter's despair and to his own bitter grief; in the romance, the father is unpleasant enough, but he temporizes and hopes rather than attempts force, and hence does not push things beyond repair. In response to a daughter's independence, Cymbeline banishes a son-in-law – a sentence that need not entail disaster and that can be revoked; but Lear turns political power over to forces of unlimited ruthlessness and thus tears a whole kingdom apart.

A very clear view of the ways in which tragedy and romance diverge is provided by the striking resemblances between *Cymbeline* and *Othello*: in each play an extremely clever man, for his own purposes, uses circumstantial evidence to persuade a husband that his new bride has been unfaithful, and the bitter and vengeful husband resolves to punish his wife by death. Though romance does not ignore evil, its vision does not include the fearful malice which, like Iago's, destroys one victim after another; instead, Iachimo's deception of Posthumus, indecent and dangerous though it is, is still a game rather than an expression of human depravity. (Shakespeare found some aspects of the basic wager plot, a folk-tale that appeared in many versions, in the ninth tale of the second day in Boccaccio's *Decameron*, others in the prose tale *Frederick of Jennen*, a sixteenth-century translation of a Dutch version of a German story.) Romance may deal with a murderous impulse, but it does not give that impulse sole and final authority; whereas Othello in his mad error goes right to work and commits murder, Posthumus uses an agent who saves him from the consequences of his own fury. It may be that Posthumus is simply lucky in having to use an agent, but it is also possible to suppose that he unconsciously chooses an unreliable murderer. In either case – cooperative circumstance or secret intent – the survival of Imogen illustrates the view, almost invariable in romance, that the hate and violence of which people are capable, however great these may be, do not necessarily achieve their destructive ends.

Romance is not watered-down tragedy; it is another way of looking at conduct and experience. It is equally aware of serious dangers to life and well-being and of preventives, safety devices, the means of return from the shadows. It does not fall short of something that might be expected of it; rather it adopts a different perspective, and the better the individual romance is, the greater its ability to persuade us of the validity of its perspective. Romance can move toward theatrical (and subliterary) hackwork, or toward dramatic (and literary) excellence. Because it affirms the saving graces of life, it may either drift toward hackneyed, mechanical happy endings or struggle toward a peace and reconciliation that have been won by hard experience. (In the present example Cymbeline, Belarius, and Imogen have suffered; Posthumus has had to undergo a painful self-contemplation.) Since "entertainment" regularly plays up the comforting aspects of character and events, romance has strong affiliations with the world of entertainment: as such it can either provide standardized gratifications or require the spectator and reader to respond sharply even amid apparently familiar fare. Traditionally, romantic entertainment includes much movement and variety, distant scene and change of scene, combat, disguise, plotting, patriotic appeal. *Cymbeline* gathers all of these in a rich amalgam of many sources: Imogen's adventures in Wales may have come from an anonymous drama of the 1580's, *Sir Clyomon and Sir Clamydes*; the Belarius materials from *Rare Triumphs of Love and Fortune*, an anonymous drama acted in 1582; the political and military "history" from Holinshed's *Chronicles*, with further details from the 1578 and 1587 editions of *The Mirror for Magistrates*. Yet out of this rather astonishing medley comes not so much formula entertainment as an entertaining but not inadequate or falsifying view of reality.

After his period of great tragedies Shakespeare turned, in his latter years in the theatre, to romance: he appears to have written *Pericles, Cymbeline, The Winter's Tale*, and *The Tempest*, roughly in that order, between 1608 and 1612. Dr Simon Forman saw a performance of *Cymbeline* at the Globe not long before September, 1611, as we know from a description of it in his manuscript "Bocke of Plaies and Notes thereof. . . ." The play need not have been new when he saw it, but the consensus of scholarly opinion, based upon its style and type, places the anterior limit of date in 1608–09. Certain elements in the late plays – the maturing of main characters, conversion or even rebirth, the triumph of justice in harmony with nature and divine ordinance – suggest to some readers that Shakespeare had personally come through a period of anguish into relative hopefulness and serenity. Though the interpretation is not implausible, we have no biographical evidence to substantiate it. What is established is that the romances were in tune with a theatrical fashion that grew strong from about 1608 on, representing in part the continual quest for novelty, in part a new exploitation of an older dramatic mode that had not been fully developed, and perhaps most of all a response to the more specialized taste of genteel audiences that for various reasons became influential at this time. Shakespeare was clearly writing in this new mode, but he developed the mode differently from the very popular John Fletcher and Fletcher's part-time collaborator, Francis Beaumont. Though *Cymbeline* itself and the Beaumont–Fletcher *Philaster* have resemblances that suggest influence in one direction or the other (a moot subject; the evidence is not conclusive), the Beaumont–Fletcher method is in general to decrease the seriousness of the political plot and to exploit to the utmost the private emotional life, sometimes by shocking events and strained or even morbid situations, and regularly by an intensified and prolonged presentation of feelings (pathos, shame, jealousy, humiliation, horror, and so on). In Shakespeare the situations, allowing for all the departures from every-day reality that are sanctioned by romance, are much less eccentric and much more representative, and the emotional life presented is not an end in itself, magnified for a slow savoring, but a natural unexpanded accompaniment of the action.

The customary procedures of romance, then, may lean toward either of two extremes: one, the escapist patterns and routines, where entertainment is expected to have no ties with truth; the other, a sophisticated sensationalism, where putting the audience through an emotional wringer drifts naturally toward off-center functionings of personality. Shakespeare's later romances are in a middle position: they stay away equally from the pure stereotypes that give little sense of what human character and experience are like, and from the whipping up of emotional states by strange situations and prolonged displays of exacerbated feeling.

Cymbeline has won, on the whole, less praise than *The Winter's Tale* and *The Tempest*. In *Cymbeline*, some readers believe, Shakespeare reveals a less sure control of his "later style": we observe looser lines, with extra syllables and more frequent feminine endings; a tendency toward solid blocking in dialogue, with more syntactical denseness and grammatical ambiguity; random outbreaks of somewhat mechanical riming. (There is still active dispute as to whether certain parts of the play, notably V, iv, 30–122, are authentic.) Some critics have argued that the plots are not well integrated, that Belarius is too sententious, that there are too many awkward expository soliloquies, that the characters are too neatly divided into black and white, that the gratifying conclusion lacks metaphysical support. On the other hand, few have failed to admire the characterization of Imogen and the ingenious construction of the last scene (V, v). Even allowing for the susceptibility of male critics to so charming and devoted a creature as Imogen, whose attractions, ranging as they do from sweetness of affection to sharpness in repartee, from blind fidelity to keen insight into motives and character, from cookery to courage, make her virtually a dream girl, there is no doubt that she is one of the most substantially characterized, and hence convincing, of Shakespeare's romantic heroines. The final revelation scene, with its unbroken, energetic, unforced movement from one disclosure to another, is one of the most skillful in all drama. Unlike Fletcher, Shakespeare does not secure his effect of almost continuous surprise by playing tricks upon the spectator, keeping him artificially in the dark and then shocking him with sudden new light. The spectator, on the contrary, knows about everything that is taking place; his surprise is simply the surprise of the characters as they make major discoveries; yet he always understands the characters. His role is not that of naive curiosity as to what is going on, or naive wonder at novelties he has not foreseen, but adult contemplation of the diverse possibilities of human nature.

The characterization of Imogen and the management of the final scene are key elements: the merits of the play lie in characterization and craftsmanship. These disclose, as the play goes on, a view of reality that carries the romance far beyond the expectable delights of painless and thoughtless entertainment.

The play is long, and an occasional scene, such as I, iv, may be somewhat drawn out, but there is an over-all vigor of movement. Though the exposition in I, i lacks finesse, the situation is introduced, and action is started, rapidly; scenes ii and iii speedily complicate the problems to be solved. In II, iii there is a good example of a scene not only providing drama in itself but pointing ahead naturally to other action: in the midst of fighting off Cloten, Imogen misses her bracelet, so that a new problem comes into view before she is finished with the one presented by Cloten. In I, vi and II, iv, which Iachimo dominates as he first tries to "seduce" Imogen and then deceives Posthumus, excellent pace and tension are created by Iachimo in his skillful maneuvers from one strategy to another. The energetic movement is supported by variety of scene; in changing locale Shakespeare can often change mood or confront us with another point of view. From the touching scene in which Pisanio tells Imogen of Posthumus' departure (I, iii) Shakespeare makes an abrupt leap to the sophistication and skepticism at Rome (I, iv), and from that back to the heavy-handed machinations of the British Queen (I, v). The courtly polish of the scene in which Imogen, in her faithful love, resists the specious appeals of Iachimo (I, vi) is followed by the rough outdoor comedy of the loutish Cloten (II, i), and this in turn by an utterly different action in Imogen's bedroom, in which danger, evil calculation, and sexual feeling are ingeniously mixed (II, ii). From the private intrigue in Rome (II, iv, v) we are thrown back to a public scene of imperial politics at the British court (III, i), and from the royal palace to an outlaws' cave in the Welsh mountains (III, iii). From sudden battlefield reversals we shift to a supernatural vision, from divine promise to death-cell ironies, from readiness for death to a reprieve (V, iii, iv).

Nothing lags; nothing stands still; the action lines hurry on, pressed by their own inner dramatic force and intermingled so expertly that something new constantly flashes into sight to alter the perspective and undercut the obvious. This is of course good entertainment in the style of romance, but it is more than that: it is a way of countering the stereotypes into which romance may slide, of announcing the variety of possibilities in human experience, and of contemplating and accepting this variety. Though variety itself may become a cliché, variety rooted in a sense of the real alternatives in feeling and action is a denial of cliché. Even in the introductory scenes Shakespeare is not willing to let Cloten be merely a laughingstock, but instead shows him through the eyes of two commentators (I, ii; II, i), the witty observer and the straight man; aside from the drama of contrast, Cloten implicitly has enough substance to attract one follower, if only a politic one. Iachimo is the treacherous Italian dear to the Elizabethan heart, but Shakespeare modifies the conventional concept of Italian character by introducing the civil and decent Philario. The vision scene in V, iv might contain only a static, decorative theophany, but Shakespeare gives it dramatic life by having the spirits attack Jupiter almost rebelliously. Belarius and his "sons" might easily be a solid family unit playing a conventional role of rustic virtue. Belarius does voice trite sentiments about the contrast between vice at court and nobility in the mountains, but in almost their first words the young men disagree; to them their cave is a prison from the world of action and knowledge (III, iii, 27 ff.). When Guiderius kills Cloten, Belarius is less laudatory than fearful (IV, ii); when Belarius wants to play safe and wait out the war, the boys override him (IV, iv). Even the boys themselves are set partly in dramatic opposition: Guiderius, the more direct and active, criticizes Arviragus, more given to savoring words and feelings, for playing Belarius' "ingenious instrument" and for drawing out his elegy for Fidele (IV, ii).

It is in the treatment of his principal characters that Shakespeare most conspicuously avoids the expected and the obvious. As masterful wife, unscrupulous mother, and sinister stepmother, the Queen is a very old and familiar character; yet Shakespeare makes her also an authentic voice of British patriotism (III, i, v). He alters the conventional villain by giving her a generally acceptable emotion; he modifies romance by observing that malicious double-dealing at court does not bar political right feeling. Cloten is defective on nearly every count: as objectionable lover, laughable "ass," and oafish courtier of dubious principles. But he too is a patriot, even though an ungraceful one (III, i, v). He is rude and overbearing to Belarius and the King's sons, but he certainly believes that he is acting in the name of the law, and he is not a coward. His dependence on his position is ludicrous, but somehow he always needs reassurance; there is a distant touch of pathos in his incompetence and hope for security, and perhaps even in his grotesque "dreams of glory" (III, v; IV, i). He tries to think, as when he expounds the cynic's view of the gold standard in moral life (II, iii, 67 ff.), or wrestles with the paradox of love and hate (III, v, 70 ff.). In other words, Cloten is complicated enough to demand more than a stereotyped response; hence the beheading may seem excessive, unpleasantly shocking. Shakespeare wants to give the audience a quick justification for the beheading; so he has Guiderius say, "Yet I not doing this, the fool had borne / My head as I do his" (IV, ii, 116–17).

Posthumus turns out to be much more than the victim of an angry king, or than the conventional romantic hero, though he is obviously to be taken as such a hero. What interests Shakespeare more than his eligibility as a lover, or his unjust banishment, is his capacity for unheroic, indeed evil, behavior : Posthumus quickly loses faith in his wife's fidelity, and then tries to arrange her murder. Romance is made to accommodate more than a little moral reality : we see both the drive for revenge and afterwards the bitter remorse. Imogen might be no more than faithful bride and pathetic victim, but Shakespeare gives her an intelligence, a spirit, and an imagination that make her seem to earn, rather than passively inherit, the good that comes her way. But he goes beyond even this achievement and at one point regards Imogen with an amused detachment that creates the most delicately ironic scene in the play. As the convention of disguise requires, Imogen takes Cloten's body for that of Posthumus, but instead of dropping the confusion at this point, Shakespeare has her go on to identify one part of the body after another as Posthumus'. Along with all the charm of her tenderness and the pathos of her apparent bereavement, there is something exquisitely comic in the assurance of her misidentifications : no one is beyond errors that evoke smiles, Shakespeare seems to say, and this implicit view makes possible a richer humanity. The impulse to humanize by stopping short of a potential idealization appears again in the final scene when Shakespeare has Imogen coolly turn her back on Lucius ("your life . . . / Must shuffle for itself," V, v, 104–05), to whom she is indebted and who is embittered by her suddenly dropping him for her own business. Shakespeare is looking at the actual ways of human nature, not at pure stereotypes. Hence, though at the end he lets Cymbeline acquire greater wisdom and dignity, he makes the king a faulty enough human being, doting on his wife, misled, capable of folly and great harshness.

Iachimo appears first as an Italian rascal, a conventional source of agreeable shudders in Renaissance England, and then apparently undergoes a pleasing conversion from skepticism to faith in chaste love. This sounds like pure theatrical hokum, but the fact is that Iachimo is a fresh and lively character. Iago, whom Iachimo strikingly resembles, has a histrionic side which is a key to Iachimo: though Iago's main pleasure, of course, is in working out his malice, he also delights in acting out the different roles that he assumes. Iachimo does not have Iago's malice, but his passion for the stage is even greater than Iago's. He loves to adopt a role and to succeed in it; he is a subtle union of actor and confidence man. Having adopted the role of disbeliever in woman's virtue, he must carry it to an extreme and conquer in it; in working on Imogen, he shifts from role to role with the agility of a born actor; in working on Posthumus, he arranges his presentation like a tight one-act play, moving from quick exposition through deepening tension to one climax and then another. Finally he chooses a very popular role, that of guilty man confessing, and here he seizes stage with an elaborate and attitudinizing self-condemnation. Even in his final five lines (V, v, 412–17) he manages to act the guilty man with a histrionic sweep, and to attract attention by praising Imogen hyperbolically.

In adopting the genre of romance, then, Shakespeare exploits all its potential variety, at one level by an always lively movement of scene and plot, and in a more fundamental way by examining characters with either an amused detachment or a fullness that stops just short of tragic complications. Though the genre commits him to solutions without disaster, he does not impose an arbitrary happy ending. His characters are complex enough to be more than flat figures of evil that perish, and of good that triumph. The characters who survive have not been merely lucky; they have been modified, have learned somewhat better or wiser ways of confronting the unexpected. The initial mood of the play is created by a widespread impulse to act resentfully and vengefully: the Queen plots deaths, the King is quick to banish, Posthumus wants Imogen killed, and Rome must punish Britain. But the closing mood is one of forbearance and generosity. Jupiter signals the change in V, iv when, though bitterly assailed by Posthumus' family, he waives his power to act punitively and actually gives promise of relief. Cymbeline can acknowledge that his trust in the Queen "was folly in me"; Lucius can rise above the harshness of the death sentence and generously ask that Fidele be saved; Cymbeline can give up a conqueror's rights and grant this request. When Iachimo confesses, Posthumus attacks himself more sharply than he does Iachimo; by relinquishing the easier course of blame, he forestalls an outbreak of recriminatory bitterness. And if the earlier Cymbeline crops up again in the royal impulse to punish Guiderius on the spot, at least now the King can wait until he knows a little more of the truth. Belarius yields up the King's sons to their father, though he is in tears at the loss of them, and Cymbeline calls Belarius "brother." The new spirit is summed up in Posthumus, who once wanted to inflict the death sentence on his wife, but who now says to Iachimo, the cause of his mad rage, "The malice [I have] towards you [is] to forgive you." It is the key line of the latter part of the play. Moved by it, Cymbeline pardons the Roman captives and then, under the further impetus of the oracle, volunteers to pay the tribute to Rome. Since the history upon which Shakespeare drew is very shadowy, and since he follows it very loosely at best, there is no reason why he should not have chosen to finish off his romance with a patriotic note of triumph that would be sure-fire theatre. Yet he chose not to make this easier appeal, but instead to ask the audience to respond in a more mature and less obvious way – to approve the acknowledgment of a national obligation to a foreign conqueror. Cymbeline's decision, since in effect it says, " We have all been wrong in Britain," is an act of humility. It marks the general triumph of magnanimity – the ultimate value dramatically espoused in the play.

But magnanimity is not unveiled in a last-minute surprise whose power to please depends upon our indifference to probability. It is rather an extension of a certain generousness that, though at times inactive, has been recurrently present. The court scenes with Lucius have always an air of courteous consideration that survives the political dispute; once even the rude Cloten approaches civility (III, i, 76 ff.). Belarius, though he kidnapped the King's sons when he was unjustly banished, did not injure or kill them; instead he brought them up in a way that could give great pleasure to the King. Belarius and Posthumus did not avenge themselves upon Cymbeline, as more persistently resentful characters might, by fighting against him in war; instead they became the instruments of his victory. Imogen has much to forgive, but she seems not even to think of the need for forgiveness.

Shakespeare defines a world in which a certain discipline of the self – which may appear as forgiveness or forbearance under provocation, or as considerateness and graciousness even in difficult relationships – is always possible and can in the end triumph, though the impulse to inflict punishment and to achieve revenge is also strong. Civility, generosity, magnanimity – such qualities mark the improved way of life that the drama reveals. It is perhaps significant that these are the virtues esteemed in another dramatic genre that was just emerging in Jacobean England and would reach its fullness three quarters of a century later – comedy of manners. We began by discussing the relation between *Cymbeline* and tragedy (the play is entitled *The Tragedie of Cymbeline* in the folio of 1623); we end by noting its affinity with comedy. The genre to which it belongs is sometimes called tragicomedy. Whether it be called tragicomedy or romance, the important point is that, in a convention which lends itself easily to an entertaining escape from reality, Shakespeare always keeps a sure foothold in human reality; that where variety is a great theatrical value, he follows the fashion brilliantly without falling into banalities; that where abnormal tensions and sensationalism could, and often did, take over, his own portrayal of violence and strong emotion did not deflect him from representative impulses and motives; and that where the popular expectation of final relief might lead to mechanical repair of disorder and restoration of well-being, Shakespeare never entirely closes off our sense of the human capacity for ill-doing. Above all, he characteristically represents an improvement in life, not as a miraculous gift to make people easily happy, but as a possession earned by the mastery, in crises, of such virtues as forbearance and magnanimity.

University of Washington   ROBERT B. HEILMAN

NOTE ON THE TEXT

Cymbeline was first published in the folio of 1623. Textual scholars are divided in their opinions about the nature of the copy used by the printers, whether it was the author's draft or a scribal transcript of it, and whether this draft or transcript had or had not been used as a theatrical prompt-book. In any case, the folio text is a reasonably good one, and it has been followed closely in the present edition. The act–scene division provided marginally for reference departs from the division of the folio at three points: I, i combining folio I, i and ii; II, iv and v dividing folio II, iv; and III, vi combining folio III, vi and vii. Departures from the folio text, except for relineations, normalization of speech-prefixes, modernization of spelling and punctuation, and correction of obvious typographical errors, are listed below with the adopted reading in italics followed by the folio reading in roman.

I, i, 4 ff. *1. Gentleman* (from here on, F assigns the speeches of the two Gentlemen simply to '1' and '2'; so also for the two Lords in I, ii, II, i, and II, iii, and for the two Captains in V, iii) 70 (F begins Scene ii here)   116 *cere* seare   143 *vile* vilde

I, iii, 9 *this* his

I, iv, 42 *offend not* offend   65 *Britain* Britanie   67 *not but* not
76 *purchase* purchases   104 *too* to   118 *thousand* thousands

I, v, 3 s.d. *Exeunt* Exit

I, vi, 28 *takes* take   98 *born* borne   104 *Fixing* Fiering   108 *by-
peeping* by peeping   147 *Solicit'st* Solicites   168 *men's* men
169 *descended* defended

II, i, 11 *curtail* curtall   31 *to-night* night   58 *husband, than*
Husband. Then   59 *make. The* make the   62 s.d. *Exit* Exeunt

II, ii, 49 *bare* beare

II, iii, 29 *vice* voyce   47 *solicits* solicity   137 *garment* Garments
154 *you* your

II, iv, 6 *hopes* hope   24 *mingled* wing-led   34 *through* thorough
36 *tenor* tenure   37 *Philario* Post.   47 *not* note   57 *you* yon
116 *one of* one   135 *the* her

II, v, 16 *German one* Iarmen on   27 *man may name* name

III, i, 20 *rocks* Oakes

III, ii, 67 *score* store   78 *nor* not

III, iii, 2 *Stoop* Sleepe   23 *robe* Babe   28 *know* knowes   83
wherein they bow whereon the Bowe

III, iv, 22 *lie* lyes   79 *afore't* a-foot   90 *make* makes   102 *eyeballs out* eyeballs

III, v, 32 *looks* looke   40 *strokes* stroke   55 s.d. *Exit* (appears
after *days* in F)   138 *insultment* insulment

III, vi, 28 (F begins Scene vii here)   57 *Whither* Whether

IV, i, 13 *imperceiverant* imperseuerant

IV, ii, 49–51 *He . . . dieter* (F assigns these lines to Arviragus)
50 *sauced* sawc'st   58 *patience* patient   71 *mountaineers* Moun-
tainers   122 *thank* thanks   154 *reck* reake   186 *ingenious* in-
genuous   205 *crare* care   206 *Might* Might'st   224 *ruddock*
Raddocke   290 *is* are   387 *an't* and't

IV, iii, 40 *betid* betide

IV, iv, 2 *find we* we find   17 *the* their   27 *hard* heard

V, i, 1 *wished* am wisht

V, iii, 24 *harts* hearts   42 *stooped* stopt   43 *they* the

V, iv, 18 *vile* vilde   29 s.d. *follow* followes   67 *geck* geeke   81
look out looke, / looke out

V, v, 64 *heard* heare   134 *On* One   198 *vilely* vildely   205 *got it*
got   252 *vile* vilde   261 *from* fro   311 *on's* one's   334 *mere*
neere   395 *brothers* Brother   405 *so* no   468 *this yet* yet this

CYMBELINE

Cymbeline, King of Britain
Cloten, son to the Queen by a former husband
Posthumus Leonatus, a gentleman, husband to Imogen
Belarius, a banished lord, disguised under the name of Morgan
Guiderius } *sons to Cymbeline, disguised under the names of*
Arviragus } *Polydore and Cadwal, supposed sons of Morgan*
Philario, friend to Posthumus }
Iachimo, friend to Philario } *Italians*
A French Gentleman, friend to Philario
Caius Lucius, General of the Roman forces
A Roman Captain
Two British Captains
Pisanio, servant to Posthumus
Cornelius, a physician
Two Lords of Cymbeline's court
Two Gentlemen of the same
Two Jailers
Queen, wife to Cymbeline
Imogen, daughter to Cymbeline by a former queen
Helen, a lady attending on Imogen
Apparitions
Lords, Ladies, Roman Senators, Tribunes, a Soothsayer,
    a Dutch Gentleman, a Spanish Gentleman, Musicians,
    Officers, Captains, Soldiers, Messengers, Attendants

Scene: *Britain, Rome*]

CYMBELINE

1. GENTLEMAN
You do not meet a man but frowns. Our bloods   1
No more obey the heavens than our courtiers
Still seem as does the King's.   3
2. GENTLEMAN   But what's the matter?
1. GENTLEMAN
His daughter, and the heir of's kingdom, whom
He purposed to his wife's sole son – a widow   5
That late he married – hath referred herself   6
Unto a poor but worthy gentleman. She's wedded,
Her husband banished, she imprisoned. All
Is outward sorrow, though I think the King
Be touched at very heart.
2. GENTLEMAN   None but the King?
1. GENTLEMAN
He that hath lost her too. So is the Queen,
That most desired the match. But not a courtier,
Although they wear their faces to the bent   13
Of the King's looks, hath a heart that is not
Glad at the thing they scowl at.
2. GENTLEMAN   And why so?
1. GENTLEMAN
He that hath missed the Princess is a thing

I, i Britain: the palace of King Cymbeline   **1** *bloods* moods   **3** *seem* ...
King's adjust their demeanor to the King's mood or expression (cf. ll.
13–14)   **5** *purposed to* intended for   **6** *referred* given   **13** *bent* tendency

Too bad for bad report, and he that hath her –
I mean, that married her, alack good man,
And therefore banished – is a creature such
As, to seek through the regions of the earth
For one his like, there would be something failing
In him that should compare. I do not think
So fair an outward and such stuff within
Endows a man but he.

24 2. GENTLEMAN   You speak him far.
　　1. GENTLEMAN
25 I do extend him, sir, within himself,
26 Crush him together rather than unfold
His measure duly.
　　2. GENTLEMAN   What's his name and birth?
　　1. GENTLEMAN
28 I cannot delve him to the root. His father
29 Was called Sicilius, who did join his honor
Against the Romans with Cassibelan,
But had his titles by Tenantius, whom
He served with glory and admired success,
33 So gained the sur-addition Leonatus;
And had, besides this gentleman in question,
Two other sons, who in the wars o' th' time
Died with their swords in hand; for which their father,
37 Then old and fond of issue, took such sorrow
That he quit being, and his gentle lady,
39 Big of this gentleman our theme, deceased
As he was born. The King he takes the babe
To his protection, calls him Posthumus Leonatus,
42 Breeds him and makes him of his bedchamber,

---

24 *speak him far* go far in praise of him　25 *extend ... himself* expand upon
his actual qualities　26–27 *Crush ... duly* diminish his worth rather than
reveal his true stature　28 *delve ... root* dig to the root of his family tree
29–31 *Sicilius, Cassibelan, Tenantius* British rulers mentioned by
Holinshed or other chroniclers　29 *did ... honor* contributed his military
fame　33 *sur-addition* added title　37 *fond of issue* loving his children　39
Big ... theme pregnant with Posthumus　42 *of his bedchamber* a member of
the royal retinue

Puts to him all the learnings that his time   43
Could make him the receiver of, which he took
As we do air, fast as 'twas minist'red,
And in's spring became a harvest, lived in court –
Which rare it is to do – most praised, most loved,
A sample to the youngest, to th' more mature   48
A glass that feated them, and to the graver   49
A child that guided dotards. To his mistress,
For whom he now is banished – her own price   51
Proclaims how she esteemed him and his virtue.
By her election may be truly read   53
What kind of man he is.

2. GENTLEMAN   I honor him
Even out of your report. But pray you tell me,
Is she sole child to th' King?

1. GENTLEMAN   His only child.
He had two sons – if this be worth your hearing,
Mark it – the eldest of them at three years old,
I' th' swathing clothes the other, from their nursery 59
Were stol'n, and to this hour no guess in knowledge   60
Which way they went.

2. GENTLEMAN   How long is this ago?

1. GENTLEMAN
Some twenty years.

2. GENTLEMAN
That a king's children should be so conveyed,   63
So slackly guarded, and the search so slow
That could not trace them!

1. GENTLEMAN   Howsoe'er 'tis strange,
Or that the negligence may well be laughed at,   66
Yet is it true, sir.

2. GENTLEMAN   I do well believe you.

---

43 *time* age   48 *sample* example   49 *feated* reflected flatteringly   51 *price* i.e. the price she paid   53 *election* choice   59 *swathing* swaddling   60 *guess in knowledge* conjecture leading to knowledge   63 *conveyed* taken away (i.e. stolen)   66 *laughed at* regarded as incredible

I. GENTLEMAN
We must forbear. Here comes the gentleman,
The Queen, and Princess.   *Exeunt.*
  Enter the Queen, Posthumus, and Imogen.

QUEEN
No, be assured you shall not find me, daughter,
After the slander of most stepmothers,
Evil-eyed unto you. You're my prisoner, but
Your jailer shall deliver you the keys

74 That lock up your restraint. For you, Posthumus,
So soon as I can win th' offended King,
I will be known your advocate. Marry, yet
The fire of rage is in him, and 'twere good

78 You leaned unto his sentence with what patience
79 Your wisdom may inform you.

POSTHUMUS   Please your Highness,
I will from hence to-day.

QUEEN   You know the peril.
81 I'll fetch a turn about the garden, pitying
The pangs of barred affections, though the King
Hath charged you should not speak together. *Exit.*

IMOGEN   O
Dissembling courtesy ! How fine this tyrant

85 Can tickle where she wounds ! My dearest husband,
I something fear my father's wrath, but nothing –

87 Always reserved my holy duty – what
His rage can do on me. You must be gone,
And I shall here abide the hourly shot
Of angry eyes, not comforted to live
But that there is this jewel in the world
That I may see again.

POSTHUMUS   My queen, my mistress.
O lady, weep no more, lest I give cause

---

74 *lock ... restraint* lock up your prison (?), lock up and restrain you (?)
78 *leaned unto* bowed to 79 *inform* equip 81 *fetch* take 85 *tickle*
(pretend to) gratify 87 *duty* i.e. as a wife; all she fears is a divorce

To be suspected of more tenderness
Than doth become a man. I will remain
The loyal'st husband that did e'er plight troth;
My residence in Rome at one Philario's,
Who to my father was a friend, to me
Known but by letter. Thither write, my queen,
And with mine eyes I'll drink the words you send,
Though ink be made of gall.

    Enter Queen.

QUEEN   Be brief, I pray you.
If the King come, I shall incur I know not
How much of his displeasure. *[aside]* Yet I'll move him
To walk this way. I never do him wrong
But he does buy my injuries, to be friends;   105
Pays dear for my offenses.   *[Exit.]*

POSTHUMUS   Should we be taking leave
As long a term as yet we have to live,
The loathness to depart would grow. Adieu.

IMOGEN
Nay, stay a little.
Were you but riding forth to air yourself,
Such parting were too petty. Look here, love;
This diamond was my mother's. Take it, heart,   *impending doom*
But keep it till you woo another wife
When Imogen is dead.

POSTHUMUS   How, how? Another?
You gentle gods, give me but this I have,
And cere up my embracements from a next   116
With bonds of death!

    [Puts on the ring.] Remain, remain thou here
While sense can keep it on. And, sweetest, fairest,
As I my poor self did exchange for you
To your so infinite loss, so in our trifles

105 *buy* accept; reward; possibly, construe as benefits (i.e. in his eyes she can do no wrong)   116 *cere up* shroud (with waxed cloth; possible pun on sealing with wax)

Imogen is imprisoned.

I still win of you. For my sake wear this.
It is a manacle of love; I'll place it
Upon this fairest prisoner.
        [Puts a bracelet on her arm.]
IMOGEN   O the gods!
When shall we see again?
        Enter Cymbeline and Lords.
POSTHUMUS   Alack, the King!
CYMBELINE
125   Thou basest thing, avoid hence, from my sight!
126   If after this command thou fraught the court
With thy unworthiness, thou diest. Away!
Thou'rt poison to my blood.
POSTHUMUS   The gods protect you,
129   And bless the good remainders of the court.
I am gone.   *Exit.*
IMOGEN   There cannot be a pinch in death
More sharp than this is.
CYMBELINE   O disloyal thing
132   That shouldst repair my youth, thou heap'st
133   A year's age on me.
IMOGEN   I beseech you, sir,
Harm not yourself with your vexation.
135   I am senseless of your wrath; a touch more rare
Subdues all pangs, all fears.
CYMBELINE   Past grace? obedience?
IMOGEN
Past hope, and in despair; that way, past grace.
CYMBELINE
That mightst have had the sole son of my queen.
IMOGEN
O blessed that I might not! I chose an eagle
140   And did avoid a puttock.

125 *avoid* go   126 *fraught* burden   129 *remainders of* those who remain at
132 *repair* restore   133 *A year's age* (perhaps 'A years' age,' i.e. an age of
years, is preferable)   135 *am senseless of* do not feel; *touch more rare* more
painful feeling   140 *puttock* kite (bird of prey; a term of contempt)

CYMBELINE
Thou took'st a beggar, wouldst have made my throne
A seat for baseness.
IMOGEN   No, I rather added
A luster to it.
CYMBELINE   O thou vile one!
IMOGEN   Sir,
It is your fault that I have loved Posthumus.
You bred him as my playfellow, and he is
A man worth any woman; overbuys me   146
Almost the sum he pays.
CYMBELINE   What, art thou mad?
IMOGEN
Almost, sir. Heaven restore me! Would I were
A neatherd's daughter, and my Leonatus   149
Our neighbor shepherd's son.
          Enter Queen.
CYMBELINE   Thou foolish thing!
          [To Queen]
They were again together. You have done
Not after our command. Away with her
And pen her up.
QUEEN   Beseech your patience. Peace,   153
Dear lady daughter, peace! Sweet sovereign,
Leave us to ourselves, and make yourself some comfort
Out of your best advice.   156
CYMBELINE   Nay, let her languish
A drop of blood a day and, being aged,
Die of this folly.   *Exit [with Lords].*
          Enter Pisanio.
QUEEN   Fie, you must give way.   158
Here is your servant. How now, sir? What news?

146–47 *overbuys ... pays* what he pays (either in giving himself or in
suffering punishment) almost entirely exceeds my value   149 *neatherd*
cowherd   153 *Beseech* I beg   156 *advice* (self-)admonition; *languish* pine
away   158 *Fie ... way* (said to Cymbeline to impress Imogen)

PISANIO

160   My lord your son drew on my master.

QUEEN   Ha!
No harm, I trust, is done?

PISANIO   There might have been
But that my master rather played than fought

163   And had no help of anger. They were parted
By gentlemen at hand.

QUEEN   I am very glad on't.

IMOGEN

165   Your son 's my father's friend ; he takes his part
To draw upon an exile. O brave sir !
I would they were in Afric both together,
Myself by with a needle that I might prick
The goer-back. Why came you from your master ?

PISANIO

170   On his command. He would not suffer me
To bring him to the haven, left these notes
Of what commands I should be subject to
When't pleased you to employ me.

QUEEN   This hath been

174   Your faithful servant. I dare lay mine honor
He will remain so.

PISANIO   I humbly thank your Highness.

QUEEN
Pray walk awhile.

IMOGEN
About some half-hour hence pray you speak with me.
You shall at least go see my lord aboard.
For this time leave me.   *Exeunt.*

*

160 *drew on* (with his sword)   163 *had ... anger* was not angry enough to fight seriously   165 *takes his part* acts as expected   170 *suffer* permit 174 *lay* wager

Enter Cloten and two Lords.   I, ii

1. LORD Sir, I would advise you to shift a shirt; the vio- 2
lence of action hath made you reek as a sacrifice. Where 2
air comes out, air comes in; there's none abroad so 3
wholesome as that you vent.

CLOTEN If my shirt were bloody, then to shift it. Have I
hurt him?

2. LORD *[aside]* No, faith, not so much as his patience.

1. LORD Hurt him? His body's a passable carcass if he be 8
not hurt. It is a throughfare for steel if it be not hurt. 9

2. LORD *[aside]* His steel was in debt. It went o' th' back- 10
side the town.

CLOTEN The villain would not stand me.   12

2. LORD *[aside]* No, but he fled forward still, toward your
face.

1. LORD Stand you? You have land enough of your own,
but he added to your having, gave you some ground.

2. LORD *[aside]* As many inches as you have oceans.
Puppies!   17

CLOTEN I would they had not come between us.

2. LORD *[aside]* So would I, till you had measured how
long a fool you were upon the ground.

CLOTEN And that she should love this fellow and refuse
me!

2. LORD *[aside]* If it be a sin to make a true election, she is 22
damned.

1. LORD Sir, as I told you always, her beauty and her
brain go not together. She's a good sign, but I have seen 25
small reflection of her wit.

2. LORD *[aside]* She shines not upon fools, lest the reflection should hurt her.

I, ii The same   2 *reek* give off vapors   3 *abroad* outside you   8 *passable*
penetrable without damage (like a fluid; with pun on meaning 'tolerable')
9 *throughfare* thoroughfare   10 *was in debt* i.e. paid back nothing   10–11
went ... town (like a debtor taking a back road; i.e. the rapier missed)   12
stand face   17 *Puppies* vain, foolish people   22 *election* choice   25 *sign*
appearance

CLOTEN Come, I'll to my chamber. Would there had been some hurt done!

2. LORD [aside] I wish not so – unless it had been the fall of an ass, which is no great hurt.

CLOTEN You'll go with us?

1. LORD I'll attend your lordship.

CLOTEN Nay, come, let's go together.

2. LORD Well, my lord.   *Exeunt.*

*

I, iii   *Enter Imogen and Pisanio.*

IMOGEN

I would thou grew'st unto the shores o' th' haven

2 And questionedst every sail. If he should write
And I not have it, 'twere a paper lost
As offered mercy is. What was the last
That he spake to thee?

PISANIO   It was his queen, his queen.

IMOGEN

Then waved his handkerchief?

PISANIO   And kissed it, madam.

IMOGEN

7 Senseless linen, happier therein than I!
And that was all?

PISANIO   No, madam. For so long
As he could make me with this eye or ear
Distinguish him from others, he did keep
The deck, with glove or hat or handkerchief
Still waving, as the fits and stirs of's mind
Could best express how slow his soul sailed on,
How swift his ship.

IMOGEN   Thou shouldst have made him

15 As little as a crow or less, ere left
To after-eye him.

I, iii The same   2–4 *If … mercy is* loss of a letter would be like loss of
mercy (offered by heaven or by king)   7 *Senseless* without feeling   15–16
ere … after-eye before you stopped gazing after

PISANIO   Madam, so I did.
IMOGEN
   I would have broke mine eyestrings, cracked them but
   To look upon him till the diminution
   Of space had pointed him sharp as my needle;
   Nay, followed him till he had melted from
   The smallness of a gnat to air, and then
   Have turned mine eye and wept. But, good Pisanio,
   When shall we hear from him?
PISANIO   Be assured, madam,
   With his next vantage.   24
IMOGEN
   I did not take my leave of him, but had
   Most pretty things to say. Ere I could tell him
   How I would think on him at certain hours
   Such thoughts and such; or I could make him swear
   The shes of Italy should not betray
   Mine interest and his honor; or have charged him
   At the sixth hour of morn, at noon, at midnight,
   T'encounter me with orisons, for then   32
   I am in heaven for him; or ere I could
   Give him that parting kiss which I had set
   Betwixt two charming words – comes in my father,   35
   And like the tyrannous breathing of the north   36
   Shakes all our buds from growing.
       Enter a Lady.
LADY   The Queen, madam,
   Desires your Highness' company.
IMOGEN
   Those things I bid you do, get them dispatched.
   I will attend the Queen.
PISANIO   Madam, I shall.   *Exeunt.*

*

24 *next vantage* first opportunity   32 *encounter ... orisons* join me in
prayers   35 *charming* magical, protecting like a charm   36 *north* north
wind

43

I, iv   *Enter Philario, Iachimo, a Frenchman, a Dutchman,*
         and a Spaniard.

IACHIMO Believe it, sir, I have seen him in Britain. He
2   was then of a crescent note, expected to prove so worthy
    as since he hath been allowed the name of. But I could
4   then have looked on him without the help of admiration,
5   though the catalogue of his endowments had been tabled
    by his side and I to peruse him by items.

PHILARIO You speak of him when he was less furnished
8   than now he is with that which makes him both without
    and within.

FRENCHMAN I have seen him in France. We had very
11 many there could behold the sun with as firm eyes as
    he.

IACHIMO This matter of marrying his king's daughter,
    wherein he must be weighed rather by her value than
14 his own, words him, I doubt not, a great deal from the
    matter.

FRENCHMAN And then his banishment.

IACHIMO Ay, and the approbation of those that weep this
18 lamentable divorce under her colors are wonderfully to
19 extend him, be it but to fortify her judgment, which else
20 an easy battery might lay flat for taking a beggar without
21 less quality. But how comes it he is to sojourn with you?
22 How creeps acquaintance?

PHILARIO His father and I were soldiers together, to
    whom I have been often bound for no less than my life.
         Enter Posthumus.
    Here comes the Briton. Let him be so entertained

I, iv Rome: the house of Philario   **2** *crescent note* growing fame   **4** *without
... admiration* without feeling wonder and respect   **5** *tabled* set down in a
list   **8** *makes* is the making of   **11** *behold the sun* (as eagles were supposed
to do; a metaphor for distinction; cf. I. i, 139–40)   **14–15** *words ... matter*
gives an account of him that goes beyond the facts   **18** *under her colors* as
supporters of Imogen   **18–19** *are ... him* have the effect of greatly
enlarging his reputation   **19** *fortify* justify   **20** *without* i.e. with (in effect,
a double negative, found more than once in Shakespeare)   **21** *quality* rank
22 *creeps* (suggests 'worming his way in')

44

amongst you as suits, with gentlemen of your knowing, to a stranger of his quality. I beseech you all be better known to this gentleman, whom I commend to you as a noble friend of mine. How worthy he is I will leave to appear hereafter, rather than story him in his own 30 hearing.

FRENCHMAN Sir, we have known together in Orleans. 31

POSTHUMUS Since when I have been debtor to you for courtesies which I will be ever to pay and yet pay still.

FRENCHMAN Sir, you o'errate my poor kindness. I was glad I did atone my countryman and you. It had been 35 pity you should have been put together with so mortal a 36 purpose as then each bore, upon importance of so slight 37 and trivial a nature.

POSTHUMUS By your pardon, sir, I was then a young traveller; rather shunned to go even with what I heard 40 than in my every action to be guided by others' experiences. But upon my mended judgment, if I offend not to 42 say it is mended, my quarrel was not altogether slight.

FRENCHMAN Faith, yes, to be put to the arbitrement of 44 swords, and by such two that would by all likelihood have confounded one the other or have fall'n both. 46

IACHIMO Can we with manners ask what was the difference?

FRENCHMAN Safely, I think. 'Twas a contention in public, which may without contradiction suffer the report. It 49 was much like an argument that fell out last night, where each of us fell in praise of our country mistresses; this 51 gentleman at that time vouching – and upon warrant of 52 bloody affirmation – his to be more fair, virtuous, wise,

---

30 *story* tell about   31 *known together* been acquainted   35 *atone* reconcile
36 *put together* i.e. in a duel   37 *importance* a matter   40 *shunned ... even*
declined to agree (cf. 'go along with')   42 *mended* improved   44 *arbitrement* settlement   46 *confounded* destroyed   49 *without ... report* without
objection be reported   51 *our country mistresses* loved women of our
countries (cf. Partridge, *Shakespeare's Bawdy*, p. 95)   52–53 *warrant ...*
affirmation pledge to support by shedding blood

54 chaste, constant, qualified, and less attemptable than
    any the rarest of our ladies in France.

    IACHIMO That lady is not now living, or this gentleman's
57 opinion, by this, worn out.

58 POSTHUMUS She holds her virtue still, and I my mind.

    IACHIMO You must not so far prefer her 'fore ours of Italy.

    POSTHUMUS Being so far provoked as I was in France, I
61 would abate her nothing, though I profess myself her
62 adorer, not her friend.

63 IACHIMO As fair and as good – a kind of hand-in-hand
    comparison – had been something too fair and too good
65 for any lady in Britain. If she went before others I have
    seen as that diamond of yours outlusters many I have
    beheld, I could not but believe she excelled many; but
    I have not seen the most precious diamond that is, nor
    you the lady.

70 POSTHUMUS I praised her as I rated her. So do I my stone.

    IACHIMO What do you esteem it at?

72 POSTHUMUS More than the world enjoys.

    IACHIMO Either your unparagoned mistress is dead, or
74 she's outprized by a trifle.

    POSTHUMUS You are mistaken. The one may be sold or
76 given, or if there were wealth enough for the purchase
    or merit for the gift. The other is not a thing for sale,
    and only the gift of the gods.

    IACHIMO Which the gods have given you?

    POSTHUMUS Which by their graces I will keep.

81 IACHIMO You may wear her in title yours, but you know
82 strange fowl light upon neighboring ponds. Your ring
83 may be stol'n too. So your brace of unprizable estima-

---

54 *qualified* having good qualities; *attemptable* vulnerable to seduction   57
by ... out by now not sound   58 *mind* opinion   61 *abate her* lower her
value (cf. 'downgrade')   62 *friend* lover, i.e. paramour   63 *hand-in-hand*
claiming equality   65 *went before* were superior to   70 *rated* estimated
72 *enjoys* possesses   74 *outprized* surpassed in value   76 *or if* either if   81
wear ... title have title to her, possess her in name   82 *ponds, ring* (see
Partridge, op. cit., pp. 169, 179)   83 *unprizable estimations* inestimable
values (cf. 'prize possessions')

tions, the one is but frail and the other casual. A cunning 84
thief, or a that-way-accomplished courtier, would hazard the winning both of first and last.

POSTHUMUS Your Italy contains none so accomplished a
courtier to convince the honor of my mistress, if, in the 88
holding or loss of that, you term her frail. I do nothing
doubt you have store of thieves; notwithstanding, I fear
not my ring.

PHILARIO Let us leave here, gentlemen.   92

POSTHUMUS Sir, with all my heart. This worthy signior,
I thank him, makes no stranger of me; we are familiar at 94
first.

IACHIMO With five times so much conversation I should
get ground of your fair mistress, make her go back even to 97
the yielding, had I admittance, and opportunity to 98
friend.

POSTHUMUS No, no.

IACHIMO I dare thereupon pawn the moiety of my estate 100
to your ring, which in my opinion o'ervalues it something. But I make my wager rather against your confidence than her reputation; and, to bar your offense
herein too, I durst attempt it against any lady in the
world.

POSTHUMUS You are a great deal abused in too bold a 105
persuasion, and I doubt not you sustain what y'are 106
worthy of by your attempt.

IACHIMO What's that?

POSTHUMUS A repulse – though your attempt, as you
call it, deserve more: a punishment too.

PHILARIO Gentlemen, enough of this. It came in too
suddenly; let it die as it was born, and I pray you be
better acquainted.

---

84 *casual* open to accident (cf. 'casualty') 88 *to convince* as to overcome
(perhaps 'convict'); *honor* chastity 92 *leave* leave off (drop the subject)
94–95 *familiar at first* on easy terms from the first 97–98 *get ground, go
back, yielding* (military and duelling terms as metaphors for sex) 98 *to* as a
100 *moiety* half 105 *abused* deceived 106 *persuasion* opinion; *sustain* will
receive

114 IACHIMO Would I had put my estate and my neighbor's
115 on th' approbation of what I have spoke!

POSTHUMUS What lady would you choose to assail?

IACHIMO Yours, whom in constancy you think stands so
safe. I will lay you ten thousand ducats to your ring that,
119 commend me to the court where your lady is, with no
120 more advantage than the opportunity of a second conference, and I will bring from thence that honor of hers
122 which you imagine so reserved.

123 POSTHUMUS I will wage against your gold, gold to it. My
ring I hold dear as my finger; 'tis part of it.

125 IACHIMO You are a friend, and therein the wiser. If you
buy ladies' flesh at a million a dram, you cannot pre-
127 serve it from tainting. But I see you have some religion
128 in you, that you fear.

129 POSTHUMUS This is but a custom in your tongue. You
bear a graver purpose, I hope.

131 IACHIMO I am the master of my speeches, and would undergo what's spoken, I swear.

POSTHUMUS Will you? I shall but lend my diamond till
134 your return. Let there be covenants drawn between's.
My mistress exceeds in goodness the hugeness of your
unworthy thinking. I dare you to this match: here's my
ring.

138 PHILARIO I will have it no lay.

IACHIMO By the gods, it is one. If I bring you no sufficient testimony that I have enjoyed the dearest bodily
part of your mistress, my ten thousand ducats are yours;
so is your diamond too. If I come off and leave her in
such honor as you have trust in, she your jewel, this
your jewel, and my gold are yours – provided I have

---

114 *put* bet   115 *on th' approbation of* that I can prove   119 *commend me*
recommend me, give me an introduction   120 *conference* meeting   122
reserved secure   123 *wage* wager; *gold to it* gold in equal amount (?)   125
You ... wiser i.e. you know her well enough to know the danger of such a
bet   127 *religion* (Iachimo sneers)   128 *that* since   129 *This* the bet, the
point of view   131 *undergo* undertake   134 *covenants* terms of agreement
138 *lay* wager

your commendation for my more free entertainment.   145
POSTHUMUS I embrace these conditions. Let us have   146
   articles betwixt us. Only, thus far you shall answer: if   147
   you make your voyage upon her and give me directly to   148
   understand you have prevailed, I am no further your
   enemy; she is not worth our debate. If she remain un-
   seduced, you not making it appear otherwise, for your
   ill opinion and the assault you have made to her chastity
   you shall answer me with your sword.
IACHIMO Your hand; a covenant. We will have these
   things set down by lawful counsel, and straight away for
   Britain, lest the bargain should catch cold and starve. I   156
   will fetch my gold and have our two wagers recorded.
POSTHUMUS Agreed.   *[Exeunt Posthumus and Iachimo.]*
FRENCHMAN Will this hold, think you?
PHILARIO Signior Iachimo will not from it. Pray let us   160
   follow 'em.   *Exeunt.*

*

Enter Queen, Ladies, and Cornelius.   I, v
QUEEN
   Whiles yet the dew 's on ground, gather those flowers.
   Make haste. Who has the note of them?   2
LADY   I, madam.
QUEEN
   Dispatch.   *Exeunt Ladies.* 3
   Now, Master Doctor, have you brought those drugs?
CORNELIUS
   Pleaseth your Highness, ay. Here they are, madam.
      [Presents a box.]
   But I beseech your Grace, without offense –

145 *commendation* recommendation, introduction; *free entertainment* **easy**
reception 146 *embrace* accept 147 *articles* terms (of the bet) 148
voyage predatory expedition (with sexual innuendo); *directly* straight-
forwardly, convincingly 156 *starve* die 160 *from it* give it up
I, v Britain: the palace of King Cymbeline 2 *note* list 3 *Dispatch* do it
quickly

49

My conscience bids me ask – wherefore you have
Commanded of me these most poisonous compounds,
9 Which are the movers of a languishing death,
But though slow, deadly.

QUEEN   I wonder, Doctor,
Thou ask'st me such a question. Have I not been
12 Thy pupil long? Hast thou not learned me how
To make perfumes? distil? preserve? yea, so
That our great king himself doth woo me oft
15 For my confections? Having thus far proceeded –
16 Unless thou think'st me devilish – is't not meet
17 That I did amplify my judgment in
18 Other conclusions? I will try the forces
Of these thy compounds on such creatures as
We count not worth the hanging – but none human –
To try the vigor of them and apply
22 Allayments to their act, and by them gather
Their several virtues and effects.

CORNELIUS   Your Highness
Shall from this practice but make hard your heart.
Besides, the seeing these effects will be
But noisome and infectious.

26 QUEEN   O, content thee.
        Enter Pisanio.
        [Aside]
Here comes a flattering rascal. Upon him
Will I first work. He's for his master,
And enemy to my son. – How now, Pisanio?
Doctor, your service for this time is ended;
Take your own way.

CORNELIUS *[aside]*   I do suspect you, madam,
But you shall do no harm.

QUEEN *[to Pisanio]*   Hark thee, a word.

9 *are ... of* cause   **12** *learned* taught   **15** *confections* compounds (drugs)
16 *meet* fitting   **17** *amplify my judgment* increase my knowledge   **18**
conclusions experiments   **22** *Allayments* antidotes; *act* action; *gather* put
together (a record of)   **26** *content thee* don't worry

CORNELIUS *[aside]*
    I do not like her. She doth think she has
    Strange ling'ring poisons. I do know her spirit
    And will not trust one of her malice with
    A drug of such damned nature. Those she has
    Will stupefy and dull the sense awhile,
    Which first perchance she'll prove on cats and dogs,
    Then afterward up higher; but there is
    No danger in what show of death it makes,   40
    More than the locking up the spirits a time,
    To be more fresh, reviving. She is fooled
    With a most false effect, and I the truer
    So to be false with her.
QUEEN   No further service, Doctor,
    Until I send for thee.
CORNELIUS   I humbly take my leave.   *Exit.*
QUEEN
    Weeps she still, say'st thou? Dost thou think in time
    She will not quench and let instructions enter   47
    Where folly now possesses? Do thou work.
    When thou shalt bring me word she loves my son,
    I'll tell thee on the instant thou art then
    As great as is thy master; greater, for
    His fortunes all lie speechless and his name
    Is at last gasp. Return he cannot nor
    Continue where he is. To shift his being   54
    Is to exchange one misery with another,
    And every day that comes comes to decay   56
    A day's work in him. What shalt thou expect
    To be depender on a thing that leans,   58
    Who cannot be new built, nor has no friends
    So much as but to prop him?
      [Drops the box. Pisanio picks it up.]
                    Thou tak'st up
    Thou know'st not what, but take it for thy labor.

47 *quench* cool down; *instructions* admonitions 54 *being* abode 56–57
comes to . . . him brings a day to nought for him 58 *leans* begins to fall

It is a thing I made which hath the King
Five times redeemed from death. I do not know
64 What is more cordial. Nay, I prithee take it.
65 It is an earnest of a farther good
66 That I mean to thee. Tell thy mistress how
The case stands with her; do't as from thyself.
68 Think what a chance thou changest on, but think
Thou hast thy mistress still – to boot, my son,
Who shall take notice of thee. I'll move the King
71 To any shape of thy preferment such
As thou'lt desire; and then myself, I chiefly,
73 That set thee on to this desert, am bound
74 To load thy merit richly. Call my women.
Think on my words.   *Exit Pisanio.*
                              A sly and constant knave,
76 Not to be shaked; the agent for his master,
77 And the remembrancer of her to hold
78 The handfast to her lord. I have given him that
Which, if he take, shall quite unpeople her
80 Of liegers for her sweet, and which she after,
81 Except she bend her humor, shall be assured
To taste of too.
          Enter Pisanio and Ladies.
82   So, so. Well done, well done.
The violets, cowslips, and the primroses
84 Bear to my closet. Fare thee well, Pisanio.
Think on my words.   *Exit Queen, and Ladies.*
PISANIO   And shall do.
But when to my good lord I prove untrue,
I'll choke myself. There's all I'll do for you.   *Exit.*

*

64 *cordial* restorative   65 *earnest* sample; token payment   66 *mean to*
intend for   68 *chance ... on* good chance (this is) to change (service)   71
shape ... preferment kind of advancement   73 *desert* meritorious action
74 *load* reward   76 *shaked* shaken (in his devotion to Posthumus)   77
remembrancer agent whose duty is to remind (legal term)   78 *handfast*
marriage contract   80 *liegers ... sweet* her husband's ambassadors   81
bend her humor change her mind   82 *So, so* good   84 *closet* room

Enter Imogen alone.

IMOGEN

A father cruel and a stepdame false,
A foolish suitor to a wedded lady
That hath her husband banished. O, that husband,
My supreme crown of grief, and those repeated   4
Vexations of it! Had I been thief-stol'n,
As my two brothers, happy; but most miserable
Is the desire that's glorious. Blessed be those,   7
How mean soe'er, that have their honest wills,   8
Which seasons comfort. Who may this be? Fie!   9

Enter Pisanio and Iachimo.

PISANIO

Madam, a noble gentleman of Rome
Comes from my lord with letters.

IACHIMO   Change you, madam: 11
The worthy Leonatus is in safety
And greets your Highness dearly.
[Presents a letter.]

IMOGEN   Thanks, good sir.
You're kindly welcome.

IACHIMO *[aside]*

All of her that is out of door most rich!   15
If she be furnished with a mind so rare,
She is alone th' Arabian bird, and I   17
Have lost the wager. Boldness be my friend!
Arm me, audacity, from head to foot,
Or like the Parthian I shall flying fight—   20
Rather, directly fly.

IMOGEN *[reads]* 'He is one of the noblest note, to whose   22

I, vi The same   4 *repeated* which I have recounted (in ll. 1–3)   7 *glorious*
for a noble thing (?), held by a person in high position (?)   8 *honest wills*
plain desires   9 *seasons* adds relish to   11 *Change you* i.e. change your
expression; I have good news   15 *out of door* visible   17 *Arabian bird*
mythical phoenix (only one existed at a time; hence, unique)   20 *Parthian*
mounted archer who fired backwards while in flight   22 *note* distinction

Iachimo - twinning, doubling
king of doublespeak

23 kindnesses I am most infinitely tied. Reflect upon him
accordingly, as you value your trust.

                         Leonatus.'

So far I read aloud.
But even the very middle of my heart
Is warmed by th' rest and takes it thankfully.
You are as welcome, worthy sir, as I
Have words to bid you, and shall find it so
In all that I can do.

IACHIMO   Thanks, fairest lady.
What, are men mad? Hath nature given them eyes
33 To see this vaulted arch and the rich crop
Of sea and land, which can distinguish 'twixt
35 The fiery orbs above and the twinned stones
36 Upon the numbered beach, and can we not
37 Partition make with spectacles so precious
'Twixt fair and foul?

38 IMOGEN   What makes your admiration?

IACHIMO
It cannot be i' th' eye, for apes and monkeys,
40 'Twixt two such shes, would chatter this way and
41 Contemn with mows the other; nor i' th' judgment,
42 For idiots, in this case of favor, would
43 Be wisely definite; nor i' th' appetite –
44 Sluttery, to such neat excellence opposed,
45 Should make desire vomit emptiness,
46 Not so allured to feed.

IMOGEN
47 What is the matter, trow?

IACHIMO   The cloyèd will –

---

23 *Reflect upon* welcome   33 *crop* harvest   35 *twinned* exactly alike   36 *numbered* (with) numerous (stones)   37 *Partition* distinction; *spectacles* eyes   38 *admiration* wonder   40 *chatter this way* speak (i.e. give approval) for this one (Imogen)   41 *mows* grimaces   42 *case of favor* question of beauty   43 *Be wisely definite* make a wise decision; *appetite* physical desire 44 *neat* elegant   45 *desire* lust; *vomit emptiness* vomit though not fed   46 *so allured* attracted by this (i.e. by *Sluttery* l. 44)   47 *trow* I wonder; *will* sexual desire

That satiate yet unsatisfied desire, that tub
Both filled and running – ravening first the lamb,   49
Longs after for the garbage.
IMOGEN   What, dear sir,
Thus raps you? Are you well?   51
IACHIMO   Thanks, madam, well.
    [*To Pisanio*]
Beseech you, sir, desire
My man's abode where I did leave him.   53
He's strange and peevish.   54
PISANIO   I was going, sir,
To give him welcome.   *Exit*.
IMOGEN
Continues well my lord? His health, beseech you?
IACHIMO
Well, madam.
IMOGEN
Is he disposed to mirth? I hope he is.
IACHIMO
Exceeding pleasant; none a stranger there
So merry and so gamesome. He is called
The Briton reveller.
IMOGEN   When he was here
He did incline to sadness, and ofttimes   62
Not knowing why.
IACHIMO   I never saw him sad.
There is a Frenchman his companion, one
An eminent monsieur that, it seems, much loves
A Gallian girl at home. He furnaces   66
The thick sighs from him, whiles the jolly Briton –   67
Your lord, I mean – laughs from's free lungs, cries 'O,
Can my sides hold to think that man who knows
By history, report, or his own proof

49 *ravening* feeding voraciously on   51 *raps* carries away   53 *man's abode*
man to await   54 *strange* a stranger; *peevish* easily distressed   62 *sadness*
seriousness   66 *Gallian* French; *furnaces* blows forth like a furnace   67
thick close together

What woman is, yea, what she cannot choose
72 But must be, will's free hours languish for
Assurèd bondage ?'

IMOGEN   Will my lord say so ?

IACHIMO
Ay, madam, with his eyes in flood with laughter.
It is a recreation to be by
And hear him mock the Frenchman. But heavens know
Some men are much to blame.

IMOGEN   Not he, I hope.

IACHIMO
78 Not he – but yet heaven's bounty towards him might
79 Be used more thankfully. In himself 'tis much ;
80 In you, which I account his, beyond all talents.
Whilst I am bound to wonder, I am bound
To pity too.

IMOGEN   What do you pity, sir ?

IACHIMO
Two creatures heartily.

IMOGEN   Am I one, sir ?

84 You look on me. What wrack discern you in me
Deserves your pity ?

IACHIMO   Lamentable ! What,
86 To hide me from the radiant sun and solace
87 I' th' dungeon by a snuff !

IMOGEN   I pray you, sir,
Deliver with more openness your answers
To my demands. Why do you pity me ?

IACHIMO
That others do,
I was about to say, enjoy your – but
92 It is an office of the gods to venge it,
Not mine to speak on 't.

---

72 *languish* give up to languishing   78 *bounty* i.e. in bestowing upon him
his own qualities, and Imogen   79 *'tis* i.e. heaven's bounty is   80 *talents*
his own qualities (?), wealth (?)   84 *wrack* wreck, disaster   86 *solace* find
pleasure   87 *snuff* partly consumed candlewick   92 *office* duty

IMOGEN   You do seem to know
Something of me or what concerns me. Pray you,
Since doubting things go ill often hurts more   95
Than to be sure they do – for certainties
Either are past remedies, or, timely knowing,   97
The remedy then born – discover to me   98
What both you spur and stop.   99

IACHIMO   Had I this cheek
To bathe my lips upon ; this hand, whose touch,
Whose every touch, would force the feeler's soul
To th' oath of loyalty ; this object, which
Takes prisoner the wild motion of mine eye,
Fixing it only here ; should I, damned then,
Slaver with lips as common as the stairs
That mount the Capitol ; join gripes with hands
Made hard with hourly falsehood (falsehood, as   107
With labor) ; then by-peeping in an eye   108
Base and illustrious as the smoky light   109
That's fed with stinking tallow – it were fit
That all the plagues of hell should at one time
Encounter such revolt.   112

IMOGEN   My lord, I fear,
Has forgot Britain.

IACHIMO   And himself. Not I   113
Inclined to this intelligence pronounce
The beggary of his change, but 'tis your graces   115
That from my mutest conscience to my tongue   116
Charms this report out.

IMOGEN   Let me hear no more.

IACHIMO
O dearest soul, your cause doth strike my heart

95 *doubting* fearing   97 *timely knowing* if one knows in time   98 *then* is
then; *discover* reveal   99 *spur and stop* prod on (toward disclosure) and
stop   107–08 *as With* as if made hard by   108 *by-peeping* looking side-
long   109 *illustrious* (for 'illustrous,' not lustrous)   112 *Encounter such
revolt* come upon (as a punishment) such inconstancy   113–14 *Not ...
pronounce* though not inclined to give this news, I report   115 *beggary*
meanness, cheapness   116 *mutest conscience* most silent knowledge

With pity that doth make me sick. A lady
120 So fair, and fastened to an empery
121 Would make the great'st king double, to be partnered
122 With tomboys hired with that self exhibition
123 Which your own coffers yield ; with diseased ventures
124 That play with all infirmities for gold
125 Which rottenness can lend nature ; such boiled stuff
As well might poison poison ! Be revenged,
Or she that bore you was no queen, and you
128 Recoil from your great stock.

IMOGEN   Revenged ?
How should I be revenged ? If this be true –
As I have such a heart that both mine ears
Must not in haste abuse – if it be true,
How should I be revenged ?

IACHIMO   Should he make me
Live like Diana's priest betwixt cold sheets,
134 Whiles he is vaulting variable ramps,
In your despite, upon your purse ? Revenge it.
I dedicate myself to your sweet pleasure,
137 More noble than that runagate to your bed,
138 And will continue fast to your affection,
139 Still close as sure.

IMOGEN   What ho, Pisanio !

IACHIMO
Let me my service tender on your lips.

IMOGEN
Away, I do condemn mine ears that have
142 So long attended thee. If thou wert honorable,
Thou wouldst have told this tale for virtue, not

120–21 *empery Would* empire which would   121–22 *partnered With tom-boys* treated the same as whores   122 *that self exhibition* the very allowance money   123 *ventures* traders (?), adventuresses (?)   124 *play* gamble, toy 125 *Which* i.e. infirmities; *boiled stuff* i.e. women treated for venereal disease by sweating   128 *Recoil ... stock* fall away from (what is natural to) your royal heredity   134 *variable ramps* various whores   137 *runagate to* truant from   138 *fast* firm   139 *close* secret   142 *attended* listened to

For such an end thou seek'st, as base as strange.
Thou wrong'st a gentleman who is as far
From thy report as thou from honor, and
Solicit'st here a lady that disdains
Thee and the devil alike. What ho, Pisanio!
The King my father shall be made acquainted
Of thy assault. If he shall think it fit
A saucy stranger in his court to mart   151
As in a Romish stew and to expound   152
His beastly mind to us, he hath a court
He little cares for and a daughter who
He not respects at all. What ho, Pisanio!

IACHIMO
O happy Leonatus! I may say
The credit that thy lady hath of thee   157
Deserves thy trust, and thy most perfect goodness   158
Her assured credit. Blessèd live you long,
A lady to the worthiest sir that ever
Country called his, and you his mistress, only   161
For the most worthiest fit. Give me your pardon.
I have spoke this to know if your affiance   163
Were deeply rooted, and shall make your lord
That which he is, new o'er; and he is one   165
The truest mannered, such a holy witch   166
That he enchants societies into him.   167
Half all men's hearts are his.

IMOGEN   You make amends.
IACHIMO
He sits 'mongst men like a descended god.
He hath a kind of honor sets him off
More than a mortal seeming. Be not angry,   171
Most mighty Princess, that I have adventured

151 *saucy* impudent; *to mart* should bargain   152 *stew* brothel   157 *credit*
... *of* faith ... in   158 *goodness* integrity (deserves)   161 *called his* called
its own   163 *affiance* loyalty   165 *new o'er* all over again (i.e. doubly so);
one above all, uniquely   166 *truest mannered* most honestly behaved; *witch*
charmer   167 *societies* social groups; *into* to   171 *mortal seeming* human
appearance

173   To try your taking of a false report, which hath
      Honored with confirmation your great judgment
175   In the election of a sir so rare,
176   Which you know cannot err. The love I bear him
177   Made me to fan you thus, but the gods made you,
178   Unlike all others, chaffless. Pray your pardon.

IMOGEN
     All's well, sir. Take my pow'r i' th' court for yours.

IACHIMO
     My humble thanks. I had almost forgot
     T' entreat your Grace but in a small request,
182   And yet of moment too, for it concerns
     Your lord, myself, and other noble friends
     Are partners in the business.

IMOGEN   Pray what is't?

IACHIMO
     Some dozen Romans of us and your lord –
     The best feather of our wing – have mingled sums
     To buy a present for the Emperor;
188   Which I, the factor for the rest, have done
     In France. 'Tis plate of rare device and jewels
     Of rich and exquisite form, their values great,
191   And I am something curious, being strange,
     To have them in safe stowage. May it please you
     To take them in protection?

IMOGEN   Willingly;
     And pawn mine honor for their safety. Since
     My lord hath interest in them, I will keep them
     In my bedchamber.

IACHIMO   They are in a trunk
     Attended by my men. I will make bold
     To send them to you, only for this night.
     I must aboard to-morrow.

IMOGEN   O, no, no.

---

173 *try your taking* test your reception   175 *election* choice   176 *Which* i.e. who   177 *fan* winnow, i.e. test   178 *chaffless* faultless   182 *moment* importance   188 *factor* agent   191 *curious* anxious; *strange* foreign

IACHIMO
   Yes, I beseech, or I shall short my word   200
   By length'ning my return. From Gallia
   I crossed the seas on purpose and on promise
   To see your Grace.
IMOGEN   I thank you for your pains.
   But not away to-morrow!
IACHIMO   O, I must, madam.
   Therefore I shall beseech you, if you please
   To greet your lord with writing, do't to-night.
   I have outstood my time, which is material   207
   To th' tender of our present.   208
IMOGEN   I will write.
   Send your trunk to me; it shall safe be kep_
   And truly yielded you. You're very welcome.   *Exeunt.*

*

    Enter Cloten and the two Lords.   II, i
CLOTEN Was there ever man had such luck? When I
   kissed the jack upon an upcast, to be hit away! I had a 2
   hundred pound on't. And then a whoreson jackanapes 3
   must take me up for swearing, as if I borrowed mine 4
   oaths of him and might not spend them at my pleasure.
1. LORD What got he by that? You have broke his pate
   with your bowl.
2. LORD *[aside]* If his wit had been like him that broke it,
   it would have run all out.
CLOTEN When a gentleman is disposed to swear, it is not
   for any standers-by to curtail his oaths. Ha?   11
2. LORD No, my lord; *[aside]* nor crop the ears of them.
CLOTEN Whoreson dog, I gave him satisfaction! Would
   he had been one of my rank.

---

200 *short* not live up to   207 *outstood* outstayed   208 *tender* giving
II, i The palace grounds   2 *kissed the jack* touched the target (in game of
bowls); *upcast* throw (?), chance (?)   3 *whoreson jackanapes* (terms of
abuse)   4 *take me up* take me to task   11 *curtail* cut down

15 2. LORD *[aside]* To have smelled like a fool.

CLOTEN I am not vexed more at anything in th' earth. A
17 pox on't! I had rather not be so noble as I am. They dare
not fight with me because of the Queen my mother.
19 Every jack-slave hath his bellyful of fighting, and I must
go up and down like a cock that nobody can match.

21 2. LORD *[aside]* You are cock and capon too, and you
crow cock with your comb on.

CLOTEN Sayest thou?

24 2. LORD It is not fit your lordship should undertake
25 every companion that you give offense to.

26 CLOTEN No, I know that, but it is fit I should commit
offense to my inferiors.

2. LORD Ay, it is fit for your lordship only.

CLOTEN Why, so I say.

1. LORD Did you hear of a stranger that's come to court
to-night?

CLOTEN A stranger, and I not know on't?

2. LORD *[aside]* He's a strange fellow himself, and knows
it not.

1. LORD There's an Italian come, and, 'tis thought, one
of Leonatus' friends.

CLOTEN Leonatus? A banished rascal, and he's another,
whatsoever he be. Who told you of this stranger?

1. LORD One of your lordship's pages.

40 CLOTEN Is it fit I went to look upon him? Is there no derogation in't?

42 2. LORD You cannot derogate, my lord.

CLOTEN Not easily, I think.

2. LORD *[aside]* You are a fool granted; therefore your
45 issues, being foolish, do not derogate.

---

15 *smelled* (pun on *rank* in l. 14)   17 *pox* venereal disease (standard oath)
19 *jack-slave* lower-class person   21–22 *capon ... on* (puns on meanings
'castration,' 'idiot,' 'coxcomb')   24 *undertake* 'take on'   25 *companion*
fellow (term of contempt)   26–27 *commit offense* attack (with excretory
pun)   40 *derogation* loss of dignity   42 *cannot derogate* i.e. have no dignity
to lose   45 *issues* acts

CLOTEN Come, I'll go see this Italian. What I have lost
   to-day at bowls I'll win to-night of him. Come, go.
2. LORD I'll attend your lordship.

Exit [Cloten with First Lord].

   That such a crafty devil as is his mother
   Should yield the world this ass ! A woman that
   Bears all down with her brain, and this her son   51
   Cannot take two from twenty, for his heart,   52
   And leave eighteen. Alas, poor princess,
   Thou divine Imogen, what thou endur'st,
   Betwixt a father by thy stepdame governed,
   A mother hourly coining plots, a wooer
   More hateful than the foul expulsion is
   Of thy dear husband, than that horrid act
   Of the divorce he'ld make. The heavens hold firm
   The walls of thy dear honor, keep unshaked
   That temple, thy fair mind, that thou mayst stand,
   T' enjoy thy banished lord and this great land !   *Exit.*

*

Enter Imogen in her bed, and a Lady [attending].   II, ii
IMOGEN
   Who's there ? My woman Helen ?
LADY   Please you, madam.
IMOGEN
   What hour is it ?
LADY   Almost midnight, madam.
IMOGEN
   I have read three hours then. Mine eyes are weak.
   Fold down the leaf where I have left. To bed.
   Take not away the taper, leave it burning ;
   And if thou canst awake by four o' th' clock,
   I prithee call me. Sleep hath seized me wholly.

                                          [Exit Lady.]

51 *Bears all down* triumphs over everything   52 *for his heart* for the life of
him
II, ii The bedchamber of Imogen

To your protection I commend me, gods.
9   From fairies and the tempters of the night,
Guard me, beseech ye!
        Sleeps. Iachimo [comes] from the trunk.
    IACHIMO
11 The crickets sing, and man's o'erlabored sense
12 Repairs itself by rest. Our Tarquin thus
13 Did softly press the rushes ere he wakened
14 The chastity he wounded. Cytherea,
15 How bravely thou becom'st thy bed, fresh lily,
And whiter than the sheets! That I might touch!
But kiss, one kiss! Rubies unparagoned,
18 How dearly they do't! 'Tis her breathing that
Perfumes the chamber thus. The flame o' th' taper
20 Bows toward her and would underpeep her lids
To see th' enclosèd lights, now canopied
22 Under these windows, white and azure-laced
23 With blue of heaven's own tinct. But my design:
To note the chamber. I will write all down:
Such and such pictures; there the window; such
26 Th' adornment of her bed; the arras, figures,
27 Why, such and such; and the contents o' th' story.
28 Ah, but some natural notes about her body
29 Above ten thousand meaner movables
Would testify, t' enrich mine inventory.
31 O sleep, thou ape of death, lie dull upon her.
32 And be her sense but as a monument,
Thus in a chapel lying. Come off, come off—
        [Takes off her bracelet.]

9 *fairies* i.e. evil fairies   11 *o'erlabored* overworked, worn out   12 *Our Tarquin* Roman who raped Lucretia   13 *rushes* floor coverings (Elizabethan)   14 *Cytherea* Venus   15 *bravely* finely; *lily* (emblem of chastity)   18 *they do't* i.e. her lips (rubies) kiss each other   20 *underpeep* peep under   22 *windows* eyelids; *azure-laced* i.e. with blue veins   23 *tinct* hue   26 *arras* tapestry   27 *story* room (?), design on arras (?)   28 *notes* marks   29 *meaner movables* less important furnishings   31 *dull* heavy   32 *monument* i.e. sculptured human form lying horizontally on a tomb

As slippery as the Gordian knot was hard.   34
'Tis mine, and this will witness outwardly,
As strongly as the conscience does within,   36
To th' madding of her lord. On her left breast   37
A mole cinque-spotted, like the crimson drops   38
I' th' bottom of a cowslip. Here's a voucher   39
Stronger than ever law could make. This secret   40
Will force him think I have picked the lock and ta'en
The treasure of her honor. No more. To what end?
Why should I write this down that's riveted,
Screwed to my memory? She hath been reading late
The tale of Tereus. Here the leaf's turned down   45
Where Philomel gave up. I have enough.
To th' trunk again, and shut the spring of it.
Swift, swift, you dragons of the night, that dawning
May bare the raven's eye. I lodge in fear.   49
Though this a heavenly angel, hell is here.
     Clock strikes.
One, two, three. Time, time!   *Exit [into the trunk].*

*

Enter Cloten and Lords.   II, iii
1. LORD Your lordship is the most patient man in loss,
   the most coldest that ever turned up ace.   2
CLOTEN It would make any man cold to lose.   3
1. LORD But not every man patient after the noble temper of your lordship. You are most hot and furious
   when you win.

34 *Gordian knot* intricate knot tied by Gordius, Phrygian king, and cut by
Alexander the Great with his sword 36 *conscience* knowledge or con-
sciousness (of Posthumus) 37 *madding* maddening 38 *cinque-spotted*
with five spots 39 *voucher* evidence 40 *secret* intimate fact 45 *Tereus*
Thracian king who raped his sister-in-law Philomela and cut out her
tongue 49 *bare...eye* (the raven was believed to wake early)
II, iii A hall adjoining Imogen's chambers 2 *coldest* coolest, calmest;
turned up ace made the lowest dice throw (with pun on 'ass') 3 *cold*
depressed

CLOTEN Winning will put any man into courage. If I
could get this foolish Imogen, I should have gold
enough. It's almost morning, is't not?

1. LORD Day, my lord.

CLOTEN I would this music would come. I am advised to
12   give her music a-mornings; they say it will penetrate.
Enter Musicians.

13   Come on, tune. If you can penetrate her with your fin-
14   gering, so; we'll try with tongue too. If none will do,
15   let her remain, but I'll never give o'er. First, a very
16   excellent good-conceited thing; after, a wonderful
sweet air with admirable rich words to it – and then let
her consider.

Song.

Hark, hark, the lark at heaven's gate sings,
20   And Phoebus gins arise,
His steeds to water at those springs
On chaliced flowers that lies;
23   And winking Mary-buds begin
To ope their golden eyes.
With every thing that pretty is,
My lady sweet, arise,
Arise, arise!

28   CLOTEN So, get you gone. If this penetrate, I will con-
29   sider your music the better; if it do not, it is a vice in her
30   ears which horsehairs and calves' guts, nor the voice of
31   unpaved eunuch to boot, can never amend.
[Exeunt Musicians.]
Enter Cymbeline and Queen.
2. LORD Here comes the King.

12, 13 *penetrate* affect emotionally (with sexual innuendo)   **14** *so* fine   **15**
give o'er give up   **16** *good-conceited* well-wrought   **20** *Phoebus* Apollo, as
the sun; *gins* begins to   **23** *winking* closed; *Mary-buds* marigold buds   **28**
consider recompense   **29** *vice* flaw   **30** *horsehairs* bowstrings; *calves' guts*
fiddle strings   **31** *unpaved* without stones (i.e. castrated)

CLOTEN I am glad I was up so late, for that's the reason I
was up so early. He cannot choose but take this service I
have done fatherly. Good morrow to your Majesty and 35
to my gracious mother.

CYMBELINE
Attend you here the door of our stern daughter?   37
Will she not forth?

CLOTEN I have assailed her with musics, but she vouch-
safes no notice.

CYMBELINE
The exile of her minion is too new;   41
She hath not yet forgot him. Some more time
Must wear the print of his remembrance on't,
And then she's yours.

QUEEN   You are most bound to th'King,
Who lets go by no vantages that may   45
Prefer you to his daughter. Frame yourself   46
To orderly solicits, and be friended   47
With aptness of the season. Make denials   48
Increase your services. So seem as if
You were inspired to do those duties which
You tender to her; that you in all obey her,
Save when command to your dismission tends,   52
And therein you are senseless.   53
CLOTEN   Senseless? Not so.
        [Enter a Messenger.]
MESSENGER
So like you, sir, ambassadors from Rome.   54
The one is Caius Lucius.
CYMBELINE   A worthy fellow,
Albeit he comes on angry purpose now.
But that's no fault of his. We must receive him

35 *fatherly* as a father (modifies *take*) 37 *Attend* wait at 41 *minion*
darling 45 *vantages* occasions 46 *Prefer* recommend; *Frame* prepare
47 *solicits* approaches, importunings 47–48 *be . . . season* make good use of
appropriate times 48 *denials* rejections (by her) 52 *dismission* dismissal
53 *are senseless* are not to understand (or obey) 54 *So like you* if you please

According to the honor of his sender,
59 And towards himself, his goodness forespent on us,
We must extend our notice. Our dear son,
When you have given good morning to your mistress,
Attend the Queen and us. We shall have need
T' employ you towards this Roman. Come, our queen.
                                    Exeunt [all but Cloten].

CLOTEN
If she be up, I'll speak with her; if not,
Let her lie still and dream. *[Knocks.]* By your leave, ho!
I know her women are about her. What
67 If I do line one of their hands? 'Tis gold
Which buys admittance – oft it doth – yea, and makes
69 Diana's rangers false themselves, yield up
70 Their deer to th' stand o' th' stealer; and 'tis gold
Which makes the true man killed and saves the thief,
Nay, sometime hangs both thief and true man. What
Can it not do and undo? I will make
One of her women lawyer to me, for
75 I yet not understand the case myself.
By your leave.
                    Knocks. Enter a Lady.

LADY
Who's there that knocks?
CLOTEN   A gentleman.
LADY   No more?
CLOTEN
Yes, and a gentlewoman's son.
LADY   That's more
Than some whose tailors are as dear as yours
Can justly boast of. What's your lordship's pleasure?
CLOTEN
81 Your lady's person. Is she ready?

---

59 *his ... us* because of his earlier goodness to us   67 *line* i.e. with money   69 *rangers* gamekeepers (i.e. attendant nymphs, vowed to chastity); *false* turn false   70 *stand* blind (hunter's station; with sexual innuendo) 75 *understand the case* know how to carry on the suit   81 *ready* dressed

LADY   Ay,
To keep her chamber.
CLOTEN   There is gold for you.
Sell me your good report.
LADY
How? My good name? Or to report of you
What I shall think is good? The Princess!
    Enter Imogen.
CLOTEN
Good morrow, fairest sister. Your sweet hand.
                           [Exit Lady.]
IMOGEN
Good morrow, sir. You lay out too much pains   87
For purchasing but trouble. The thanks I give
Is telling you that I am poor of thanks
And scarce can spare them.
CLOTEN   Still I swear I love you.
IMOGEN
If you but said so, 'twere as deep with me.   91
If you swear still, your recompense is still   92
That I regard it not.
CLOTEN   This is no answer.
IMOGEN
But that you shall not say I yield being silent,   94
I would not speak. I pray you spare me. Faith,
I shall unfold equal discourtesy   96
To your best kindness. One of your great knowing   97
Should learn, being taught, forbearance.
CLOTEN
To leave you in your madness, 'twere my sin.
I will not.
IMOGEN
Fools are not mad folks.
CLOTEN   Do you call me fool?

87 *lay out* expend   91 *deep* effective   92 *still* continually   94 *But that* in order that   96 *unfold* show   97 *knowing* knowledge (ironic)

IMOGEN
    As I am mad, I do.
    If you'll be patient, I'll no more be mad ;
    That cures us both. I am much sorry, sir,
    You put me to forget a lady's manners
106   By being so verbal ; and learn now for all
    That I, which know my heart, do here pronounce
    By th' very truth of it, I care not for you,
    And am so near the lack of charity
110   To accuse myself I hate you – which I had rather
    You felt than make't my boast.

CLOTEN   You sin against
112   Obedience, which you owe your father. For
113   The contract you pretend with that base wretch,
    One bred of alms and fostered with cold dishes,
    With scraps o' th' court – it is no contract, none.
116   And though it be allowed in meaner parties –
    Yet who than he more mean ? – to knit their souls,
118   On whom there is no more dependency
119   But brats and beggary, in self-figured knot ;
120   Yet you are curbed from that enlargement by
121   The consequence o' th' crown, and must not foil
122   The precious note of it with a base slave,
123   A hilding for a livery, a squire's cloth,
124   A pantler – not so eminent.

IMOGEN   Profane fellow !
    Wert thou the son of Jupiter, and no more
    But what thou art besides, thou wert too base
127   To be his groom. Thou wert dignified enough,

---

106 *verbal* talkative, i.e. Cloten (?), outspoken, i.e. Imogen (?)　110 *To ... hate* that I must accuse myself of hating　112 *For* as for　113 *contract* i.e. of marriage; *pretend* offer as an excuse (for not having me)　116 *meaner parties* lower-class people　118 *On ... dependency* with no other consequence　119 *self-figured* self-arranged　120 *curbed ... enlargement* restrained from that freedom　121 *consequence* what follows (from your inheritance); *foil* foul　122 *note* distinction　123 *hilding* good-for-nothing; *for ... cloth* suited for servant's attire　124 *pantler* pantry man; *not* not even　127 *dignified* given honor

Even to the point of envy, if 'twere made   128
Comparative for your virtues to be styled
The under-hangman of his kingdom, and hated
For being preferred so well.
CLOTEN   The south fog rot him!   131
IMOGEN
He never can meet more mischance than come
To be but named of thee. His meanest garment   133
That ever hath but clipped his body is dearer   134
In my respect than all the hairs above thee,   135
Were they all made such men. How now, Pisanio?   136
      Enter Pisanio.
CLOTEN
'His garment'? Now the devil –
IMOGEN
To Dorothy my woman hie thee presently.
CLOTEN
'His garment'?
IMOGEN   I am sprited with a fool,   139
Frighted, and ang'red worse. Go bid my woman
Search for a jewel that too casually
Hath left mine arm. It was thy master's. Shrew me   142
If I would lose it for a revenue
Of any king's in Europe. I do think
I saw't this morning; confident I am
Last night 'twas on mine arm; I kissed it.
I hope it be not gone to tell my lord
That I kiss aught but he.
PISANIO   'Twill not be lost.
IMOGEN
I hope so. Go and search.   *[Exit Pisanio.]* 149

128–30 *if ... kingdom* if, according to the virtue of each of you, you were
made under-hangman and he king   131 *south fog* south wind, supposedly
damp and unhealthful   133 *of* by   134 *clipped* embraced   135 *respect*
regard   136 *How now* (Imogen suddenly notices that the bracelet is
gone)   139 *sprited* haunted   142 *Shrew* curse (mild, polite oath; here
used emphatically)   149 *so* i.e. not

71

CLOTEN   You have abused me.
'His meanest garment'?

IMOGEN   Ay, I said so, sir.
151   If you will make't an action, call witness to't.

CLOTEN
I will inform your father.

IMOGEN   Your mother too.
153   She's my good lady and will conceive, I hope,
But the worst of me. So I leave you, sir,
To th' worst of discontent.   *Exit.*

CLOTEN   I'll be revenged.
'His meanest garment'? Well.   *Exit.*

*

II, iv   *Enter Posthumus and Philario.*

POSTHUMUS
Fear it not, sir. I would I were so sure
2   To win the King as I am bold her honor
Will remain hers.

3 PHILARIO   What means do you make to him?

POSTHUMUS
Not any, but abide the change of time,
5   Quake in the present winter's state, and wish
6   That warmer days would come. In these feared hopes
7   I barely gratify your love; they failing,
I must die much your debtor.

PHILARIO
Your very goodness and your company
10   O'erpays all I can do. By this, your king
Hath heard of great Augustus; Caius Lucius
Will do's commission throughly. And I think
13   He'll grant the tribute, send th' arrearages,

151 *action* lawsuit   153 *conceive* think, believe
II, iv Rome: the house of Philario   2 *bold* certain   3 *means* approaches
5 *winter's* i.e. bitter, outcast   6 *feared* fear-laden   7 *gratify* repay   10 *this*
now   13 *He* Cymbeline; *arrearages* overdue payments of tribute

Or look upon our Romans, whose remembrance   14
Is yet fresh in their grief.   15
POSTHUMUS   I do believe,
Statist though I am none, nor like to be,   16
That this will prove a war ; and you shall hear   17
The legion now in Gallia sooner landed
In our not-fearing Britain than have tidings
Of any penny tribute paid. Our countrymen
Are men more ordered than when Julius Caesar   21
Smiled at their lack of skill but found their courage
Worthy his frowning at. Their discipline,
Now mingled with their courages, will make known
To their approvers they are people such   25
That mend upon the world.   26
    Enter Iachimo.
PHILARIO   See, Iachimo!
POSTHUMUS
The swiftest harts have posted you by land,   27
And winds of all the corners kissed your sails   28
To make your vessel nimble.
PHILARIO   Welcome, sir.
POSTHUMUS
I hope the briefness of your answer made   30
The speediness of your return.
IACHIMO   Your lady
Is one of the fairest that I have looked upon.
POSTHUMUS
And therewithal the best, or let her beauty
Look through a casement to allure false hearts
And be false with them.
IACHIMO   Here are letters for you.

14 *Or* or else (?), before, rather than (?)   15 *their* the Britons' (as caused by
the Romans)   16 *Statist* statesman   17 *prove* result in, turn out to be   21
ordered disciplined   25 *approvers* those who test them   26 *mend upon*
improve   27 *have posted* must have sped   28 *corners* quarters   30 *your
answer* (Imogen's) reply to you

POSTHUMUS
   Their tenor good, I trust.
36 IACHIMO   'Tis very like.
PHILARIO
   Was Caius Lucius in the Briton court
   When you were there?
IACHIMO   He was expected then,
   But not approached.
POSTHUMUS   All is well yet.
   Sparkles this stone as it was wont, or is't not
   Too dull for your good wearing?
IACHIMO   If I have lost it,
   I should have lost the worth of it in gold.
   I'll make a journey twice as far t'enjoy
   A second night of such sweet shortness which
   Was mine in Britain – for the ring is won.
POSTHUMUS
   The stone's too hard to come by.
IACHIMO   Not a whit,
   Your lady being so easy.
POSTHUMUS   Make not, sir,
   Your loss your sport. I hope you know that we
   Must not continue friends.
IACHIMO   Good sir, we must,
50 If you keep covenant. Had I not brought
51 The knowledge of your mistress home, I grant
52 We were to question farther, but I now
   Profess myself the winner of her honor,
   Together with your ring, and not the wronger
   Of her or you, having proceeded but
   By both your wills.
POSTHUMUS   If you can make't apparent
   That you have tasted her in bed, my hand
   And ring is yours. If not, the foul opinion
   You had of her pure honor gains or loses

36 *like* likely 50 *keep covenant* hold to the bargain 51 *knowledge* i.e
sexual 52 *question* dispute in a duel

74

Your sword or mine, or masterless leave both   60
To who shall find them.
IACHIMO   Sir, my circumstances,   61
Being so near the truth as I will make them,
Must first induce you to believe; whose strength   63
I will confirm with oath, which I doubt not
You'll give me leave to spare when you shall find   65
You need it not.
POSTHUMUS   Proceed.
IACHIMO   First, her bedchamber –
Where I confess I slept not, but profess
Had that was well worth watching – it was hanged   68
With tapestry of silk and silver; the story
Proud Cleopatra, when she met her Roman
And Cydnus swelled above the banks, or for   71
The press of boats or pride : a piece of work
So bravely done, so rich, that it did strive   73
In workmanship and value; which I wondered
Could be so rarely and exactly wrought,
Since the true life on't was –
POSTHUMUS   This is true,
And this you might have heard of here, by me
Or by some other.
IACHIMO   More particulars
Must justify my knowledge.   79
POSTHUMUS   So they must,
Or do your honor injury.
IACHIMO   The chimney
Is south the chamber, and the chimney piece   81
Chaste Dian bathing. Never saw I figures
So likely to report themselves. The cutter   83

60 *leave* let it leave (some editors emend to 'leaves') 61 *circumstances*
circumstantial report 63 *whose* (antecedent is *circumstances*) 65 *spare*
omit 68 *watching* staying awake 71 *Cydnus* river where Antony and
Cleopatra met 71–72 *or ... press* either because of the multitude 73
bravely finely 73–74 *did ... value* it was a question whether form or
content was better 79 *justify* prove 81 *south* on the south wall of; *piece*
art work 83 *likely to report* able to identify; *cutter* sculptor

84 Was as another nature, dumb; outwent her,
85 Motion and breath left out.

POSTHUMUS   This is a thing
86 Which you might from relation likewise reap,
    Being, as it is, much spoke of.

IACHIMO   The roof o' th' chamber
88 With golden cherubins is fretted. Her andirons –
89 I had forgot them – were two winking Cupids
    Of silver, each on one foot standing, nicely
91 Depending on their brands.

POSTHUMUS   This is her honor!
    Let it be granted you have seen all this – and praise
    Be given to your remembrance – the description
94 Of what is in her chamber nothing saves
    The wager you have laid.

IACHIMO   Then, if you can
    [Shows the bracelet.]
96 Be pale, I beg but leave to air this jewel. See!
97 And now 'tis up again. It must be married
    To that your diamond; I'll keep them.

POSTHUMUS   Jove!
    Once more let me behold it. Is it that
    Which I left with her?

IACHIMO   Sir, I thank her, that.
    She stripped it from her arm; I see her yet.
102 Her pretty action did outsell her gift,
    And yet enriched it too. She gave it me and said
    She prized it once.

POSTHUMUS   May be she plucked it off
    To send it me.

IACHIMO   She writes so to you, doth she?

---

84 *as ... dumb* like nature (in creative power) but unable to make a
sculpture speak; *outwent her* surpassed nature   85 *Motion ... out* i.e. the
sculptor cannot move or breathe   86 *from ... reap* learn at second hand
88 *fretted* adorned by carvings   89 *winking* with eyes closed (i.e. blind)
91 *Depending ... brands* leaning on their torches   94 *nothing saves* by no
means wins   96 *Be pale* stay unflushed (i.e. calm)   97 *up* put up (i.e. in
his pocket)   102 *outsell* exceed in value

POSTHUMUS

  O, no, no, no, 'tis true. Here, take this too.
    [Gives the ring.]
  It is a basilisk unto mine eye,   107
  Kills me to look on't. Let there be no honor
  Where there is beauty ; truth, where semblance ; love,
  Where there's another man. The vows of women   110
  Of no more bondage be to where they are made
  Than they are to their virtues, which is nothing.
  O, above measure false !

PHILARIO   Have patience, sir,
  And take your ring again ; 'tis not yet won.
  It may be probable she lost it, or   115
  Who knows if one of her women, being corrupted,
  Hath stol'n it from her ?

POSTHUMUS   Very true,
  And so I hope he came by't. Back my ring ;   118
  Render to me some corporal sign about her
  More evident than this, for this was stol'n.   120

IACHIMO

  By Jupiter, I had it from her arm.

POSTHUMUS

  Hark you, he swears ; by Jupiter he swears.
  'Tis true – nay, keep the ring – 'tis true. I am sure
  She would not lose it. Her attendants are
  All sworn and honorable. They induced to steal it ?   125
  And by a stranger ? No, he hath enjoyed her.
  The cognizance of her incontinency   127
  Is this. She hath bought the name of whore thus dearly. 128
  There, take thy hire, and all the fiends of hell   129
  Divide themselves between you !

PHILARIO   Sir, be patient.

---

107 *basilisk* mythical reptile, believed to kill by look   **110–11** *The vows …
made* let women's vows no more bind them to men   **115** *probable*
provable   **118** *so* in this manner   **120** *More evident* which is better
evidence   **125** *sworn* bound (as if) by oath   **127** *cognizance* identifying
mark   **128** *this* i.e. the ring   **129** *hire* winnings

This is not strong enough to be believed
132   Of one persuaded well of.
POSTHUMUS   Never talk on't.
133   She hath been colted by him.
IACHIMO   If you seek
For further satisfying, under her breast —
Worthy the pressing — lies a mole, right proud
Of that most delicate lodging. By my life,
137   I kissed it, and it gave me present hunger
To feed again, though full. You do remember
139   This stain upon her?
POSTHUMUS   Ay, and it doth confirm
140   Another stain, as big as hell can hold,
Were there no more but it.
IACHIMO   Will you hear more?
POSTHUMUS
142   Spare your arithmetic; never count the turns.
Once, and a million!
IACHIMO   I'll be sworn.
POSTHUMUS   No swearing.
If you will swear you have not done't, you lie,
And I will kill thee if thou dost deny
Thou'st made me cuckold.
IACHIMO   I'll deny nothing.
POSTHUMUS
147   O that I had her here, to tear her limb-meal!
I will go there and do't i' th' court, before
Her father. I'll do something.   *Exit*.
149 PHILARIO   Quite besides
The government of patience! You have won.
151   Let's follow him and pervert the present wrath
He hath against himself.
IACHIMO   With all my heart.   *Exeunt*.

---

132 *persuaded well of* well thought of   **133** *been colted by* had intercourse with   **137** *present* immediate   **139** *stain* mark, discoloration   **140** *stain* moral flaw   **142** *turns* occasions, deviations   **147** *limb-meal* limb from limb   **149–50** *besides The government* beyond the control   **151** *pervert* turn aside

Enter Posthumus.   II, v

POSTHUMUS

Is there no way for men to be, but women   1
Must be half-workers? We are all bastards, (men)   2
And that most venerable man which I
Did call my father was I know not where
When I was stamped. Some coiner with his tools   5
Made me a counterfeit; yet my mother seemed
The Dian of that time. So doth my wife
The nonpareil of this. O, vengeance, vengeance!
Me of my lawful pleasure she restrained
And prayed me oft forbearance – did it with   *embarrassment*
A pudency so rosy, the sweet view on't   11
Might well have warmed old Saturn – that I thought her   12
As chaste as unsunned snow. O, all the devils!
This yellow Iachimo in an hour, was't not?   14
Or less? At first? Perchance he spoke not, but,   15
Like a full-acorned boar, a German one,   16
Cried 'O!' and mounted; found no opposition
But what he looked for should oppose and she
Should from encounter guard. Could I find out
The woman's part in me! For there's no motion   20
That tends to vice in man but I affirm
It is the woman's part. Be it lying, note it,
The woman's; flattering, hers; deceiving, hers;
Lust and rank thoughts, hers, hers; revenges, hers;
Ambitions, covetings, change of prides, disdain,   25
Nice longings, slanders, mutability,   26
All faults that man may name, nay, that hell knows,
Why, hers, in part or all, but rather all.
For even to vice

II, v 1 *be* exist 2 *half-workers* i.e. in begetting 5 *stamped* minted (i.e. begotten) 8 *nonpareil* one without equal 11 *pudency* modesty 12 *Saturn* (this god was thought to be cold and gloomy; cf. 'saturnine') 14 *yellow* i.e. in complexion 15 *At first* immediately 16 *full-acorned* full of acorns; *German* (allusion not clear) 20–21 *motion . . . to* impulse toward 25 *change of prides* series of vanities 26 *Nice* finicky or lascivious; *mutability* fickleness

They are not constant, but are changing still
One vice but of a minute old for one
Not half so old as that. I'll write against them,
Detest them, curse them. Yet 'tis greater skill
In a true hate to pray they have their will;
The very devils cannot plague them better.   *Exit.*

*

III, i   *Enter in state Cymbeline, Queen, Cloten, and*
              Lords at one door, and at another, Caius Lucius and
              Attendants.

CYMBELINE
Now say, what would Augustus Caesar with us?

LUCIUS
When Julius Caesar, whose remembrance yet
Lives in men's eyes and will to ears and tongues
Be theme and hearing ever, was in this Britain
And conquered it, Cassibelan thine uncle,
Famous in Caesar's praises no whit less
Than in his feats deserving it, for him
And his succession granted Rome a tribute,
Yearly three thousand pounds, which by thee lately
Is left untendered.

10 QUEEN   And, to kill the marvel,
Shall be so ever.

CLOTEN   There be many Caesars
Ere such another Julius. Britain's a world
By itself, and we will nothing pay
For wearing our own noses.

QUEEN   That opportunity
15 Which then they had to take from's, to resume
We have again. Remember, sir, my liege,
The kings your ancestors, together with

III, i Britain: a room of state in the palace of King Cymbeline   10 *kill the marvel* eliminate the surprise (i.e. when non-payment is standard procedure)   15 *resume* take back

The natural bravery of your isle, which stands
As Neptune's park, ribbèd and palèd in   19
With rocks unscalable and roaring waters,
With sands that will not bear your enemies' boats   21
But suck them up to th' topmast. A kind of conquest
Caesar made here, but made not here his brag
Of 'Came and saw and overcame.' With shame,
The first that ever touched him, he was carried
From off our coast, twice beaten; and his shipping,
Poor ignorant baubles on our terrible seas,   27
Like eggshells moved upon their surges, cracked
As easily 'gainst our rocks. For joy whereof
The famed Cassibelan, who was once at point –   30
O giglet fortune! – to master Caesar's sword,   31
Made Lud's town with rejoicing fires bright   32
And Britons strut with courage.

CLOTEN Come, there's no more tribute to be paid. Our
kingdom is stronger than it was at that time, and, as I
said, there is no moe such Caesars. Other of them may
have crook'd noses, but to owe such straight arms, none. 37

CYMBELINE
Son, let your mother end.

CLOTEN We have yet many among us can gripe as hard as 39
Cassibelan. I do not say I am one, but I have a hand.
Why tribute? Why should we pay tribute? If Caesar can
hide the sun from us with a blanket or put the moon in
his pocket, we will pay him tribute for light; else, sir, no
more tribute, pray you now.

CYMBELINE
You must know,
Till the injurious Romans did extort   46
This tribute from us, we were free. Caesar's ambition,

---

19 *ribbèd* enclosed; *palèd* fenced   21 *sands* i.e quicksands   27 *ignorant*
silly, inexperienced   30–31 *at point . . . to master* on the point . . . of
mastering   31 *giglet* wanton, promiscuous   32 *Lud's town* London (after
Lud, legendary king)   37 *crook'd* i.e. Roman (cf. l. 14); *owe* own   39 *gripe*
grip (in combat)   46 *injurious* insolent

81

Which swelled so much that it did almost stretch
49   The sides o' th' world, against all color here
Did put the yoke upon's ; which to shake off
Becomes a warlike people, whom we reckon
52   Ourselves to be, we do. Say then to Caesar,
53   Our ancestor was that Mulmutius which
Ordained our laws, whose use the sword of Caesar
55   Hath too much mangled, whose repair and franchise
Shall, by the power we hold, be our good deed,
Though Rome be therefore angry. Mulmutius made our
    laws,
Who was the first of Britain which did put
His brows within a golden crown and called
Himself a king.
LUCIUS   I am sorry, Cymbeline,
61   That I am to pronounce Augustus Caesar –
62   Caesar, that hath moe kings his servants than
Thyself domestic officers – thine enemy.
64   Receive it from me then : war and confusion
In Caesar's name pronounce I 'gainst thee. Look
For fury not to be resisted. Thus defied,
I thank thee for myself.
CYMBELINE   Thou art welcome, Caius.
Thy Caesar knighted me ; my youth I spent
Much under him ; of him I gathered honor,
70   Which he to seek of me again, perforce,
71   Behooves me keep at utterance. I am perfect
72   That the Pannonians and Dalmatians for
Their liberties are now in arms, a precedent
74   Which not to read would show the Britons cold.

49 *against all color* without any justifying pretext (with pun on 'collar';
note *yoke* in l. 50)   52 *we do* i.e. shake off (some editors begin the next
sentence with 'we do')   53 *Mulmutius* earlier king, told about in
chronicles   55 *whose* (the antecedent is *laws*); *franchise* free exercise   61
pronounce declare   62 *moe* more; *his* as his   64 *confusion* destruction   70
he to seek since he seeks it; *perforce* of necessity   71 *keep at utterance* to
defend to the uttermost; *perfect* well aware   72 *Pannonians and Dalmatians* inhabitants of present-day Balkan regions   74 *cold* lacking spirit

So Caesar shall not find them.

LUCIUS   Let proof speak.   75

CLOTEN His Majesty bids you welcome. Make pastime
with us a day or two, or longer. If you seek us afterwards in other terms, you shall find us in our salt-water
girdle; if you beat us out of it, it is yours. If you fall in
the adventure, our crows shall fare the better for you,
and there's an end.

LUCIUS So, sir.

CYMBELINE I know your master's pleasure, and he
mine. All the remain is, welcome.   *Exeunt.* 84

*

Enter Pisanio, reading of a letter.   III, ii

PISANIO
How? Of adultery? Wherefore write you not
What monsters her accuse? Leonatus,
O master, what a strange infection
Is fall'n into thy ear! What false Italian,
As poisonous tongued as handed, hath prevailed
On thy too ready hearing? Disloyal? No.
She's punished for her truth and undergoes,   7
More goddess-like than wife-like, such assaults
As would take in some virtue. O my master,   9
Thy mind to her is now as low as were   10
Thy fortunes. How? That I should murder her,
Upon the love and truth and vows which I
Have made to thy command? I her? Her blood?
If it be so to do good service, never
Let me be counted serviceable. How look I
That I should seem to lack humanity
So much as this fact comes to? *[Reads]* 'Do't! The letter 17
That I have sent her, by her own command

75 *Let proof speak* let the military test settle it   84 *the remain* that remains
III, ii A chamber in the palace   7 *truth* fidelity; *undergoes* bears   9 *take in*
conquer   10 *to* compared with   17 *fact* deed

Shall give thee opportunity.' O damned paper,
20 Black as the ink that's on thee! Senseless bauble,
21 Art thou a fedary for this act, and look'st
So virgin-like without? Lo, here she comes.
    Enter Imogen.
23 I am ignorant in what I am commanded.

IMOGEN
How now, Pisanio?

PISANIO
Madam, here is a letter from my lord.

IMOGEN
Who, thy lord? That is my lord Leonatus?
27 O, learn'd indeed were that astronomer
28 That knew the stars as I his characters;
He'ld lay the future open. You good gods,
30 Let what is here contained relish of love,
31 Of my lord's health, of his content – yet not
That we two are asunder; let that grieve him.
33 Some griefs are med'cinable; that is one of them,
34 For it doth physic love – of his content
35 All but in that. Good wax, thy leave. Blessed be
36 You bees that make these locks of counsel. Lovers
37 And men in dangerous bonds pray not alike;
38 Though forfeiters you cast in prison, yet
39 You clasp young Cupid's tables. Good news, gods!
    [Reads.]
40 'Justice and your father's wrath, should he take me in
41 his dominion, could not be so cruel to me as you, O the
dearest of creatures, would even renew me with your

---

20 *Senseless bauble* inanimate trifle   **21** *fedary for* confederate in   **23** *am ignorant* will pretend ignorance   **27** *astronomer* astrologer   **28** *characters* handwriting   **30** *relish* taste   **31** *not* not content   **33** *are med'cinable* have medicinal value   **34** *physic* medicate; increase the strength of   **35** *wax* i.e. in the seal of the letter   **36** *locks of counsel* seals for confidential matters   **37** *in ... bonds* under bonds imposing penalties; *pray not alike* i.e. lovers adore, bonded men hate, waxen seals   **38** *forfeiters* those who do not live up to bonds   **39** *clasp ... tables* fasten love letters   **40** *take* capture   **41–42** *as ... renew* that you could not restore

eyes. Take notice that I am in Cambria at Milford   43
Haven. What your own love will out of this advise you,
follow. So he wishes you all happiness that remains
loyal to his vow, and your increasing in love.   46
                              Leonatus Posthumus.'
O, for a horse with wings! Hear'st thou, Pisanio?
He is at Milford Haven. Read, and tell me
How far 'tis thither. If one of mean affairs   50
May plod it in a week, why may not I
Glide thither in a day? Then, true Pisanio,
Who long'st like me to see thy lord, who long'st—
O, let me bate—but not like me, yet long'st,   54
But in a fainter kind—O, not like me!
For mine's beyond beyond: say, and speak thick—   56
Love's counsellor should fill the bores of hearing, 57
To th' smothering of the sense—how far it is   58
To this same blessèd Milford. And by th' way   59
Tell me how Wales was made so happy as
T'inherit such a haven. But first of all,
How we may steal from hence, and for the gap   62
That we shall make in time from our hence-going
And our return, to excuse. But first, how get hence?
Why should excuse be born or ere begot?   65
We'll talk of that hereafter. Prithee speak,
How many score of miles may we well rid   67
'Twixt hour and hour?
PISANIO   One score 'twixt sun and sun,
Madam, 's enough for you, and too much too.
IMOGEN
Why, one that rode to's execution, man,
Could never go so slow. I have heard of riding wagers 71
Where horses have been nimbler than the sands

43 *Cambria* Wales   46 *increasing* (object of *wishes*)   50 *mean affairs* trivial
business   54 *bate* abate, tone down (the statement)   56 *thick* fast   57 *counsellor* helper; *bores of hearing* ears   58 *To . . . sense* and even overwhelm the
hearing   59 *by th' way* on the way   62–64 *for . . . excuse* how to account for
the elapsed time, etc.   65 *or ere begot* i.e. before it is made necessary by
what we do   67 *rid* get rid of, cover   71 *riding wagers* racing bets

73 That run i' th' clock's behalf. But this is fool'ry.
    Go bid my woman feign a sickness, say
75 She'll home to her father ; and provide me presently
    A riding suit, no costlier than would fit
77 A franklin's housewife.
PISANIO   Madam, you're best consider.
IMOGEN
78 I see before me, man. Nor here, nor here,
79 Nor what ensues, but have a fog in them
    That I cannot look through. Away, I prithee ;
    Do as I bid thee. There's no more to say.
    Accessible is none but Milford way.   *Exeunt.*

*

III, iii   *Enter [from their cave] Belarius, Guiderius, and*
                Arviragus.
BELARIUS
1   A goodly day not to keep house with such
    Whose roof 's as low as ours ! Stoop, boys. This gate
3   Instructs you how t' adore the heavens and bows you
4   To a morning's holy office. The gates of monarchs
5   Are arched so high that giants may jet through
    And keep their impious turbans on without
    Good morrow to the sun. Hail, thou fair heaven !
8   We house i' th' rock, yet use thee not so hardly
9   As prouder livers do.
GUIDERIUS   Hail, heaven !
ARVIRAGUS   Hail, heaven !
BELARIUS
    Now for our mountain sport. Up to yond hill ;

73 *i' th' clock's behalf* i.e. in an hourglass   75 *home* go home; *presently*
without delay   77 *franklin* freeholder (small land-owner); *you're best* you
had better   78 *before me* i.e. the road to Milford; *Nor ... here* i.e. neither
to right nor to left   79 *what ensues* the eventual outcome
III, iii Wales: before the cave of Belarius   1 *keep house* stay in   3 *bows you*
makes you bow   4 *holy office* religious service   5 *jet* strut   8 *use* treat;
hardly badly   9 *prouder livers* people who live more resplendently

Your legs are young. I'll tread these flats. Consider,
When you above perceive me like a crow,
That it is place which lessens and sets off,   13
And you may then revolve what tales I have told you
Of courts, of princes, of the tricks in war.
This service is not service, so being done,   16
But being so allowed. To apprehend thus   17
Draws us a profit from all things we see,
And often, to our comfort, shall we find
The sharded beetle in a safer hold   20
Than is the full-winged eagle. O, this life
Is nobler than attending for a check,   22
Richer than doing nothing for a robe,   23
Prouder than rustling in unpaid-for silk:
Such gain the cap of him that makes him fine   25
Yet keeps his book uncrossed. No life to ours.   26

GUIDERIUS
Out of your proof you speak. We poor unfledged   27
Have never winged from view o' th' nest, nor know not
What air 's from home. Haply this life is best   29
If quiet life be best, sweeter to you
That have a sharper known, well corresponding
With your stiff age; but unto us it is
A cell of ignorance, travelling abed,   33
A prison, or a debtor that not dares
To stride a limit.   35
ARVIRAGUS   What should we speak of
When we are old as you? When we shall hear
The rain and wind beat dark December, how

---

13 *place* position; *sets off* embellishes 16 *This* any act of 17 *allowed*
acknowledged; *To . . . thus* to look at things in this way 20 *sharded* with
scaly wing covers; *hold* stronghold 22 *attending . . . check* doing service (at
court) only to get a rebuke 23 *robe* i.e. of office 25 *gain . . . fine* is
respected by the elegant man 26 *keeps . . . uncrossed* does not cross off
(pay the debts in) his record-book (possibly, tailor) 27 *proof* experience
29 *air's* the air is like; *from* away from; *Haply* perhaps 33 *abed* i.e. in
imagination 35 *stride a limit* cross a boundary (and thus risk arrest)

38 In this our pinching cave shall we discourse
The freezing hours away ? We have seen nothing.
40 We are beastly : subtle as the fox for prey,
41 Like warlike as the wolf for what we eat.
Our valor is to chase what flies. Our cage
We make a choir, as doth the prisoned bird,
And sing our bondage freely.

BELARIUS   How you speak!
Did you but know the city's usuries
And felt them knowingly ; the art o' th' court,
47 As hard to leave as keep, whose top to climb
Is certain falling, or so slipp'ry that
The fear 's as bad as falling ; the toil o' th' war,
50 A pain that only seems to seek out danger
51 I' th' name of fame and honor, which dies i' th' search
And hath as oft a sland'rous epitaph
53 As record of fair act ; nay, many times
54 Doth ill deserve by doing well ; what's worse,
Must curtsy at the censure. O boys, this story
The world may read in me. My body 's marked
57 With Roman swords, and my report was once
58 First with the best of note. Cymbeline loved me,
And when a soldier was the theme, my name
Was not far off. Then was I as a tree
Whose boughs did bend with fruit. But in one night
A storm or robbery, call it what you will,
63 Shook down my mellow hangings, nay, my leaves,
And left me bare to weather.

GUIDERIUS   Uncertain favor!
BELARIUS
My fault being nothing, as I have told you oft,
66 But that two villains, whose false oaths prevailed

---

38 *pinching* i.e. with cold   40 *beastly* beast-like   41 *Like* as   47 *keep* stay
in   50 *pain* labor   51 *which* (the antecedent may be *pain* or *fame and
honor*)   53 *fair act* fine deed   54 *deserve* earn, get   57 *report* reputation
58 *best of note* most distinguished   63 *hangings* fruit   66–67 *prevailed
Before* had more weight than

Before my perfect honor, swore to Cymbeline
I was confederate with the Romans. So
Followed my banishment, and this twenty years
This rock and these demesnes have been my world,   70
Where I have lived at honest freedom, paid   71
More pious debts to heaven than in all
The fore-end of my time. But up to th' mountains!   73
This is not hunters' language. He that strikes
The venison first shall be the lord o' th' feast;
To him the other two shall minister,
And we will fear no poison, which attends   77
In place of greater state. I'll meet you in the valleys.
                  Exeunt [Guiderius and Arviragus].
How hard it is to hide the sparks of nature!
These boys know little they are sons to th' King,
Nor Cymbeline dreams that they are alive.
They think they are mine, and though trained up thus
    meanly
I' th' cave wherein they bow, their thoughts do hit   83
The roofs of palaces, and nature prompts them
In simple and low things to prince it much   85
Beyond the trick of others. This Polydore,   86
The heir of Cymbeline and Britain, who
The King his father called Guiderius – Jove!
When on my three-foot stool I sit and tell
The warlike feats I have done, his spirits fly out   90
Into my story; say 'Thus mine enemy fell,   91
And thus I set my foot on's neck,' even then
The princely blood flows in his cheek, he sweats,
Strains his young nerves, and puts himself in posture   94
That acts my words. The younger brother Cadwal,
Once Arviragus, in as like a figure   96

---

70 *demesnes* regions   71 *at* in   73 *fore-end ... time* early part of my life
77 *attends* is to be expected   83–84 *do hit ... palaces* i.e. are elevated,
aspire greatly   85 *prince it* act like a prince   86 *trick* aptitude   90–91 *fly
out Into* (cf. 'empathize')   91 *say* (parallel with *tell* in l. 89)   94 *nerves*
sinews   96 *in ... figure* with an equally good acting out

Strikes life into my speech and shows much more
98 His own conceiving. Hark, the game is roused!
O Cymbeline, heaven and my conscience knows
Thou didst unjustly banish me; whereon,
At three and two years old, I stole these babes,
Thinking to bar thee of succession as
103 Thou reft'st me of my lands. Euriphile,
Thou wast their nurse; they took thee for their mother,
105 And every day do honor to her grave.
Myself, Belarius, that am Morgan called,
107 They take for natural father. The game is up.   *Exit.*

*

III, iv   *Enter Pisanio and Imogen.*

IMOGEN
1 Thou told'st me, when we came from horse, the place
Was near at hand. Ne'er longed my mother so
3 To see me first as I have now. Pisanio, man,
Where is Posthumus? What is in thy mind
That makes thee stare thus? Wherefore breaks that sigh
From th' inward of thee? One but painted thus
7 Would be interpreted a thing perplexed
Beyond self-explication. Put thyself
9 Into a havior of less fear, ere wildness
10 Vanquish my staider senses. What's the matter?
Why tender'st thou that paper to me with
12 A look untender? If't be summer news,
13 Smile to't before; if winterly, thou need'st
But keep that count'nance still. My husband's hand?
15 That drug-damned Italy hath outcraftied him,

98 *conceiving* interpretation; *roused* flushed   103 *reft'st* robbed   105 *her*
i.e. Euriphile's   107 *game is up* (repeats l. 98)
III, iv An open place near Milford Haven   1 *came from horse* dismounted
3 *have* i.e. longing to see Posthumus   7 *perplexed* troubled   9 *havior . . .
fear* less frightening demeanor; *wildness* panic   10 *staider senses* more
balanced feelings   12, 13 *summer, winterly* good, bad   15 *drug-damned*
cursed by the use of drugs; *outcraftied* been too crafty for

And he's at some hard point. Speak, man! Thy tongue   16
May take off some extremity, which to read   17
Would be even mortal to me.   18

PISANIO   Please you read,
And you shall find me, wretched man, a thing
The most disdained of fortune.

IMOGEN [reads] 'Thy mistress, Pisanio, hath played the
strumpet in my bed, the testimonies whereof lie bleeding in me. I speak not out of weak surmises, but from
proof as strong as my grief and as certain as I expect my
revenge. That part thou, Pisanio, must act for me, if thy
faith be not tainted with the breach of hers. Let thine   26
own hands take away her life. I shall give thee opportunity at Milford Haven – she hath my letter for the
purpose – where, if thou fear to strike and to make me
certain it is done, thou art the pander to her dishonor
and equally to me disloyal.'

PISANIO
What shall I need to draw my sword? The paper
Hath cut her throat already. No, 'tis slander,
Whose edge is sharper than the sword, whose tongue
Outvenoms all the worms of Nile, whose breath   35
Rides on the posting winds and doth belie   36
All corners of the world. Kings, queens, and states, 37
Maids, matrons, nay, the secrets of the grave
This viperous slander enters. What cheer, madam?

IMOGEN
False to his bed? What is it to be false?
To lie in watch there and to think on him?   41
To weep 'twixt clock and clock? If sleep charge nature, 42
To break it with a fearful dream of him   43
And cry myself awake? That's false to's bed, is it?

16 *hard point* (cf. 'tough spot')   17 *take ... extremity* reduce the extreme
painfulness (of the news)   18 *mortal* fatal   26 *tainted* contaminated   35
worms serpents   36 *posting* speeding; *belie* spread lies over   37 *states*
people of national importance   41 *in watch* awake   42 *'twixt ... clock*
from hour to hour; *charge* burden   43 *fearful ... him* dream involving fear
for him

PISANIO
  Alas, good lady!
IMOGEN
46 I false? Thy conscience witness! Iachimo,
  Thou didst accuse him of incontinency.
  Thou then lookedst like a villain; now, methinks,
49 Thy favor's good enough. Some jay of Italy,
50 Whose mother was her painting, hath betrayed him.
  Poor I am stale, a garment out of fashion,
52 And, for I am richer than to hang by th' walls,
  I must be ripped. To pieces with me! O,
54 Men's vows are women's traitors! All good seeming,
55 By thy revolt, O husband, shall be thought
56 Put on for villainy, not born where't grows,
  But worn a bait for ladies.
PISANIO   Good madam, hear me.
IMOGEN
58 True honest men, being heard like false Aeneas,
59 Were in his time thought false, and Sinon's weeping
60 Did scandal many a holy tear, took pity
  From most true wretchedness. So thou, Posthumus,
62 Wilt lay the leaven on all proper men;
63 Goodly and gallant shall be false and perjured
64 From thy great fail. Come, fellow, be thou honest;
  Do thou thy master's bidding. When thou seest him,
66 A little witness my obedience. Look,
  I draw the sword myself. Take it, and hit
  The innocent mansion of my love, my heart.

---

46 *Thy* i.e. Posthumus'   49 *favor* countenance; *jay* whore   50 *Whose ... painting* i.e. produced by painting, not by nature; *false*   52 *for ... than* since I'm too rich   54 *seeming* appearance   55 *By thy revolt* because of thy turning away (infidelity)   56 *born* i.e. natural   58 *heard* i.e. heard to speak; *false Aeneas* (he deserted Dido)   59 *Sinon* (who won the confidence of the Trojans by complaining of his treatment at the hands of his fellow Greeks, and was thus able to persuade them to admit the wooden horse, in which Greek warriors were concealed)   60 *scandal* discredit   62 *lay ... men* destroy confidence in honest men   63 *be* i.e. seem   64 *From ... fail* because of your falseness   66 *witness* testify to

Fear not, 'tis empty of all things but grief.
Thy master is not there, who was indeed
The riches of it. Do his bidding, strike!
Thou mayst be valiant in a better cause,
But now thou seem'st a coward.

PISANIO   Hence, vile instrument!
Thou shalt not damn my hand.

IMOGEN   Why, I must die,
And if I do not by thy hand, thou art
No servant of thy master's. Against self-slaughter
There is a prohibition so divine
That cravens my weak hand. Come, here's my heart –   78
Something's afore't; soft, soft, we'll no defense –   79
Obedient as the scabbard. What is here?   80
The scriptures of the loyal Leonatus   81
All turned to heresy? Away, away,
Corrupters of my faith! You shall no more
Be stomachers to my heart.   84
      [Takes his letters out of her bodice.]
                                    Thus may poor fools
Believe false teachers. Though those that are betrayed
Do feel the treason sharply, yet the traitor
Stands in worse case of woe.   87
And thou, Posthumus, that didst set up   88
My disobedience 'gainst the King my father
And make me put into contempt the suits
Of princely fellows, shalt hereafter find
It is no act of common passage, but   92
A strain of rareness; and I grieve myself
To think, when thou shalt be disedged by her   94
That now thou tirest on, how thy memory   95

78 *cravens* makes cowardly   79 *Something* i.e. Posthumus' letter, which she
speaks of as if it were armor   80 *Obedient* i.e. in receiving the sword   81
scriptures letter (with pun on 'Scriptures')   84 *stomachers* decorative
breast-coverings   87 *Stands . . . woe* is worse off   88 *set up* spur, push
92–93 *It . . . rareness* my choice was not an every-day occurrence but the
result of a rare trait   94 *disedged* dulled (in sexual desire)   95 *tirest on*
devourest (like a bird of prey)

96   Will then be panged by me. Prithee dispatch,
        The lamb entreats the butcher. Where's thy knife?
        Thou art too slow to do thy master's bidding
        When I desire it too.

PISANIO   O gracious lady,
        Since I received command to do this business
        I have not slept one wink.

IMOGEN   Do't, and to bed then.

PISANIO
102   I'll wake mine eyeballs out first.

IMOGEN   Wherefore then
103   Didst undertake it? Why hast thou abused
        So many miles with a pretense? This place?
        Mine action and thine own? Our horses' labor?
        The time inviting thee? The perturbed court
        For my being absent? whereunto I never
        Purpose return. Why hast thou gone so far,
109   To be unbent when thou hast ta'en thy stand,
110   Th' elected deer before thee?

PISANIO   But to win time
111   To lose so bad employment, in the which
        I have considered of a course. Good lady,
        Hear me with patience.

IMOGEN   Talk thy tongue weary, speak.
        I have heard I am a strumpet, and mine ear,
115   Therein false struck, can take no greater wound,
116   Nor tent to bottom that. But speak.

PISANIO   Then, madam,
117   I thought you would not back again.

IMOGEN   Most like,
        Bringing me here to kill me.

PISANIO   Not so, neither.

---

96 *panged* made miserable   102 *wake ... out* stay awake until my eyeballs
come out   103 *abused* made bad use of   109 *unbent* i.e. not shooting (the
figure is that of a bow)   110 *elected* chosen   111 *which* (the antecedent is
time)   115 *take* receive   116 *tent ... that* probe that (wound) to its depths
117 *back* go back

94

But if I were as wise as honest, then
My purpose would prove well. It cannot be
But that my master is abused. Some villain,   121
Ay, and singular in his art, hath done you both   122
This cursèd injury.

IMOGEN
Some Roman courtesan.

PISANIO   No, on my life.   124
I'll give but notice you are dead, and send him
Some bloody sign of it, for 'tis commanded
I should do so. You shall be missed at court,
And that will well confirm it.   128

IMOGEN   Why, good fellow,
What shall I do the while? Where bide? How live?
Or in my life what comfort when I am
Dead to my husband?

PISANIO   If you'll back to th' court –

IMOGEN
No court, no father, nor no more ado
With that harsh, noble, simple nothing,
That Cloten, whose love suit hath been to me
As fearful as a siege.

PISANIO   If not at court,
Then not in Britain must you bide.

IMOGEN   Where then?
Hath Britain all the sun that shines? Day, night,
Are they not but in Britain? I' th' world's volume
Our Britain seems as of it, but not in't;   139
In a great pool a swan's nest. Prithee think
There's livers out of Britain.   141

PISANIO   I am most glad
You think of other place. Th' ambassador,
Lucius the Roman, comes to Milford Haven
To-morrow. Now if you could wear a mind

121 *abused* deceived   122 *singular* without equal   124 *No . . . life* (repeats
his assertion of l. 118)   128 *it* i.e. your death   139 *of . . . in't* belonging to
it but separated from it   141 *livers* people who live

95

145 Dark as your fortune is, and but disguise
146 That which, t' appear itself, must not yet be
147 But by self-danger, you should tread a course
148 Pretty and full of view; yea, happily, near
The residence of Posthumus, so nigh, at least,
That though his actions were not visible, yet
151 Report should render him hourly to your ear
As truly as he moves.

IMOGEN   O, for such means,
153 Though peril to my modesty, not death on't,
I would adventure.

PISANIO   Well then, here's the point:
You must forget to be a woman; change
156 Command into obedience, fear and niceness –
The handmaids of all women, or more truly
158 Woman it pretty self – into a waggish courage;
159 Ready in gibes, quick-answered, saucy, and
160 As quarrelous as the weasel. Nay, you must
Forget that rarest treasure of your cheek,
162 Exposing it – but O, the harder heart!
Alack, no remedy – to the greedy touch
164 Of common-kissing Titan, and forget
165 Your laborsome and dainty trims, wherein
166 You made great Juno angry.

IMOGEN   Nay, be brief.
167 I see into thy end and am almost
A man already.

PISANIO   First, make yourself but like one.

---

145 *Dark* unrecognizable 146 *That* i.e. her sex; *t'appear* if it be revealed
147 *tread* i.e. pursue 148 *Pretty ... view* desirable, with good prospects;
happily (probably for 'haply': perhaps) 151 *render* give information
about 153 *modesty* chastity 156 *Command* i.e. her prerogative as the
King's daughter; *niceness* fastidiousness 158 *it* its; *waggish* roguish 159
quick-answered quick in reply 160 *quarrelous* quarrelsome 162 *harder*
too hard (different editors regard this as applying to Posthumus, Pisanio,
or Imogen herself) 164 *Of ... Titan* of the sun who kisses everything
165 *laborsome ... trims* elaborate and tasteful attire 166 *angry* i.e. with
jealousy 167 *end* purpose, plan

Forethinking this, I have already fit –   169
'Tis in my cloak-bag – doublet, hat, hose, all
That answer to them. Would you, in their serving,   171
And with what imitation you can borrow
From youth of such a season, 'fore noble Lucius   173
Present yourself, desire his service, tell him   174
Wherein you're happy, which will make him know,   175
If that his head have ear in music; doubtless
With joy he will embrace you, for he's honorable,   177
And, doubling that, most holy. Your means abroad –   178
You have me, rich, and I will never fail
Beginning nor supplyment.

IMOGEN   Thou art all the comfort
The gods will diet me with. Prithee away.
There's more to be considered, but we'll even   182
All that good time will give us. This attempt
I am soldier to, and will abide it with   184
A prince's courage. Away, I prithee.

PISANIO

Well, madam, we must take a short farewell,
Lest, being missed, I be suspected of
Your carriage from the court. My noble mistress,   188
Here is a box; I had it from the Queen.
What's in't is precious. If you are sick at sea
Or stomach-qualmed at land, a dram of this
Will drive away distemper. To some shade,   192
And fit you to your manhood. May the gods   193
Direct you to the best.

IMOGEN   Amen. I thank thee.   *Exeunt.*

*

169 *Forethinking* planning for in advance; *fit* prepared   171 *answer to* match; *in their serving* with their assistance   173 *season* age   174 *his service* to work for him   175 *happy* gifted; *make him know* be convincing to him (?)   177 *embrace* receive   178 *means* i.e. of subsistence   182 *even* keep up with   184 *am soldier to* have courage for; *abide* face   188 *Your carriage* taking you away   192 *distemper* illness   193 *fit you to* dress yourself for

97

III, v　　　　　*Enter Cymbeline, Queen, Cloten, Lucius, and Lords.*

CYMBELINE
Thus far, and so farewell.

LUCIUS　　　　　　　　　　Thanks, royal sir.
My emperor hath wrote I must from hence,
And am right sorry that I must report ye
My master's enemy.

CYMBELINE　　　　　　Our subjects, sir,
Will not endure his yoke, and for ourself
To show less sovereignty than they, must needs
Appear unkinglike.

LUCIUS　　　　　　　　　So, sir. I desire of you
8　　A conduct overland to Milford Haven.
Madam, all joy befall your Grace, and you.

CYMBELINE
10　　My lords, you are appointed for that office;
The due of honor in no point omit.
So farewell, noble Lucius.

LUCIUS　　　　　　　　　　Your hand, my lord.

CLOTEN
Receive it friendly, but from this time forth
I wear it as your enemy.

14 LUCIUS　　　　　　　　Sir, the event
Is yet to name the winner. Fare you well.

CYMBELINE
Leave not the worthy Lucius, good my lords,
Till he have crossed the Severn. Happiness!
　　　　　　　　　　　　　　　　Exit Lucius &c.

QUEEN
18　　He goes hence frowning, but it honors us
That we have given him cause.

CLOTEN　　　　　　　　　　'Tis all the better;
20　　Your valiant Britons have their wishes in it.

III, v The palace of Cymbeline　8 *conduct* escort　10 *office* duty　14
event outcome　18 *it honors us* it is to our credit (i.e. we have been
patriotic)　20 *have . . . it* i.e. approve our course

CYMBELINE
Lucius hath wrote already to the Emperor
How it goes here. It fits us therefore ripely   22
Our chariots and our horsemen be in readiness.
The pow'rs that he already hath in Gallia
Will soon be drawn to head, from whence he moves   25
His war for Britain.

QUEEN   'Tis not sleepy business,   26
But must be looked to speedily and strongly.

CYMBELINE
Our expectation that it would be thus
Hath made us forward. But, my gentle queen,   29
Where is our daughter? She hath not appeared
Before the Roman, nor to us hath tendered
The duty of the day. She looks us like   32
A thing more made of malice than of duty.
We have noted it. Call her before us, for
We have been too slight in sufferance.   35
                              [Exit a Messenger.]

QUEEN   Royal sir,
Since the exile of Posthumus, most retired   36
Hath her life been; the cure whereof, my lord,
'Tis time must do. Beseech your Majesty,
Forbear sharp speeches to her. She's a lady
So tender of rebukes that words are strokes,   40
And strokes death to her.
          Enter a Messenger.

CYMBELINE   Where is she, sir? How
Can her contempt be answered?   42

MESSENGER   Please you, sir,
Her chambers are all locked, and there's no answer
That will be given to th' loud of noise we make.   44

---

22 *fits* befits; *ripely* fully (cf. 'the time is ripe')   25 *drawn to head*
organized, mobilized   26 *sleepy* sleep-permitting (cf. 'asleep on the job')
29 *forward* (take) early (action)   32 *us* to us   35 *slight in sufferance* weak in
tolerance (of her conduct)   36 *retired* withdrawn, unsocial   40 *tender of*
sensitive to   42 *answered* accounted for   44 *loud* loudness (some editors
emend *loud of* to 'loudest')

QUEEN
My lord, when last I went to visit her,
46 She prayed me to excuse her keeping close;
47 Whereto constrained by her infirmity,
She should that duty leave unpaid to you
Which daily she was bound to proffer. This
50 She wished me to make known, but our great court
51 Made me to blame in memory.

CYMBELINE   Her doors locked?
Not seen of late? Grant, heavens, that which I fear
Prove false!   *Exit.*

QUEEN   Son, I say, follow the King.

CLOTEN
That man of hers, Pisanio, her old servant,
I have not seen these two days.

QUEEN   Go, look after. *Exit [Cloten].*
56 Pisanio, thou that stand'st so for Posthumus—
He hath a drug of mine. I pray his absence
58 Proceed by swallowing that, for he believes
It is a thing most precious. But for her,
60 Where is she gone? Haply despair hath seized her,
Or, winged with fervor of her love, she's flown
To her desired Posthumus. Gone she is
To death or to dishonor, and my end
Can make good use of either. She being down,
I have the placing of the British crown.
          Enter Cloten.
How now, my son?

CLOTEN   'Tis certain she is fled.
Go in and cheer the King. He rages; none
Dare come about him.

QUEEN *[aside]*   All the better. May
69 This night forestall him of the coming day!   *Exit.*

---

46 *close* to herself   47 *constrained* compelled; *infirmity* ill-being, poor
condition   50 *great court* important session of court   51 *to blame* faulty
56 *stand'st so for* so strongly support   58 *Proceed by* result from   60
Haply perhaps   69 *forestall* deprive

CLOTEN
I love and hate her, for she's fair and royal,   70
And that she hath all courtly parts more exquisite   71
Than lady, ladies, woman. From every one
The best she hath, and she, of all compounded,
Outsells them all. I love her therefore, but   74
Disdaining me and throwing favors on   75
The low Posthumus slanders so her judgment   76
That what's else rare is choked ; and in that point   77
I will conclude to hate her, nay, indeed,
To be revenged upon her. For, when fools
Shall –
        Enter Pisanio.
            Who is here ? What, are you packing, sirrah ?   80
Come hither. Ah, you precious pander ! Villain,
Where is thy lady ? In a word, or else
Thou art straightway with the fiends.

PISANIO   O good my lord !

CLOTEN
Where is thy lady ? Or – by Jupiter,
I will not ask again. Close villain,   85
I'll have this secret from thy heart, or rip
Thy heart to find it. Is she with Posthumus ?
From whose so many weights of baseness cannot
A dram of worth be drawn.   89

PISANIO   Alas, my lord,
How can she be with him ? When was she missed ?
He is in Rome.

CLOTEN   Where is she, sir ? Come nearer.   91
No farther halting. Satisfy me home   92
What is become of her.

PISANIO
O my all-worthy lord !

70 *for* because   71 *that* because; *parts* qualities   74 *Outsells* outvalues
75 *Disdaining* her disdaining   76 *slanders* disgraces   77 *what's else rare*
her other rare qualities   80 *packing* plotting   85 *Close* secretive   89
drawn extracted   91 *nearer* i.e. to the point   92 *home* completely

CLOTEN   All-worthy villain!

95 Discover where thy mistress is at once,
At the next word. No more of 'worthy lord'!

97 Speak, or thy silence on the instant is
Thy condemnation and thy death.

PISANIO   Then, sir,
This paper is the history of my knowledge

100 Touching her flight.
     [Presents a letter.]

CLOTEN   Let's see't. I will pursue her
Even to Augustus' throne.

101 PISANIO *[aside]*   Or this, or perish.
She's far enough, and what he learns by this

103 May prove his travel, not her danger.

CLOTEN   Humh!

PISANIO *[aside]*
I'll write to my lord she's dead. O Imogen,
Safe mayst thou wander, safe return again!

CLOTEN Sirrah, is this letter true?

PISANIO Sir, as I think.

CLOTEN It is Posthumus' hand; I know't. Sirrah, if thou

109 wouldst not be a villain, but do me true service, undergo
those employments wherein I should have cause to use

111 thee with a serious industry – that is, what villainy soe'er
I bid thee do, to perform it directly and truly – I would
think thee an honest man. Thou shouldst neither want

114 my means for thy relief nor my voice for thy preferment.

PISANIO Well, my good lord.

CLOTEN Wilt thou serve me? For since patiently and constantly thou hast stuck to the bare fortune of that beggar

118 Posthumus, thou canst not, in the course of gratitude,
but be a diligent follower of mine. Wilt thou serve me?

---

95 *Discover* reveal   97–98 *silence ... condemnation* silence will condemn
you instantly   100 *Touching* concerning   101 *Or* either   103 *travel* difficulty, trouble   109 *undergo* undertake   111 *industry* application   114
relief assistance; *voice* support; *preferment* advancement   118 *course*
ordinary action

PISANIO Sir, I will.

CLOTEN Give me thy hand. Here's my purse. Hast any of thy late master's garments in thy possession?

PISANIO I have, my lord, at my lodging the same suit he wore when he took leave of my lady and mistress.

CLOTEN The first service thou dost me, fetch that suit hither. Let it be thy first service. Go.

PISANIO I shall, my lord.   *Exit.*

CLOTEN Meet thee at Milford Haven! I forgot to ask him one thing; I'll remember't anon. Even there, thou villain Posthumus, will I kill thee. I would these garments were come. She said upon a time – the bitterness of it I now belch from my heart – that she held the very garment of Posthumus in more respect than my noble and natural person, together with the adornment of my qualities. With that suit upon my back will I ravish her; 135 first kill him, and in her eyes. There shall she see my valor, which will then be a torment to her contempt. He 137 on the ground, my speech of insultment ended on his 138 dead body, and when my lust hath dined – which, as I say, to vex her I will execute in the clothes that she so praised – to the court I'll knock her back, foot her home 141 again. She hath despised me rejoicingly, and I'll be merry in my revenge.

Enter Pisanio [with the clothes].

Be those the garments?

PISANIO Ay, my noble lord.

CLOTEN How long is't since she went to Milford Haven?

PISANIO She can scarce be there yet.

CLOTEN Bring this apparel to my chamber; that is the second thing that I have commanded thee. The third is that thou wilt be a voluntary mute to my design. Be but 150 duteous, and true preferment shall tender itself to thee.

---

135 *qualities* talents 137 *to her contempt* to her because of her contempt for me 138 *insultment* triumph and scorn 141 *foot* kick 150 *be . . . mute to* be willing to keep quiet about (as if mute)

My revenge is now at Milford. Would I had wings to
follow it ! Come, and be true.   *Exit.*

PISANIO

154   Thou bid'st me to my loss, for true to thee
Were to prove false, which I will never be,
156   To him that is most true. To Milford go,
And find not her whom thou pursuest. Flow, flow,
You heavenly blessings, on her. This fool's speed
159   Be crossed with slowness ; labor be his meed.   *Exit.*

*

III, vi   *Enter Imogen alone [in boy's clothes].*

IMOGEN

I see a man's life is a tedious one.
I have tired myself, and for two nights together
Have made the ground my bed. I should be sick
But that my resolution helps me. Milford,
When from the mountain top Pisanio showed thee,
6   Thou wast within a ken. O Jove, I think
7   Foundations fly the wretched – such, I mean,
Where they should be relieved. Two beggars told me
I could not miss my way. Will poor folks lie,
That have afflictions on them, knowing 'tis
11   A punishment or trial ? Yes. No wonder,
12   When rich ones scarce tell true. To lapse in fulness
13   Is sorer than to lie for need, and falsehood
Is worse in kings than beggars. My dear lord,
Thou art one o' th' false ones. Now I think on thee
16   My hunger 's gone, but even before, I was
17   At point to sink for food. But what is this ?

---

154 *to my loss* to lose my honor   156 *him* i.e. Posthumus, whom Pisanio
thinks misled rather than untrue   159 *crossed* thwarted ; *meed* reward
III, vi Wales: before the cave of Belarius   6 *ken* sight   7 *Foundations*
(pun on the meanings 'security' and 'charitable organizations')   11 *trial*
test (of faith or moral quality)   12 *lapse in fulness* lie when well-to-do   13
sorer worse   16 *even* just   17 *At point* about ; *for* for lack of

Here is a path to't. 'Tis some savage hold.   18
I were best not call; I dare not call. Yet famine,   19
Ere clean it o'erthrow nature, makes it valiant.   20
Plenty and peace breeds cowards; hardness ever   21
Of hardiness is mother. Ho! Who's here?   22
If anything that's civil, speak; if savage,
Take or lend. Ho! No answer? Then I'll enter.   24
Best draw my sword, and if mine enemy
But fear the sword like me, he'll scarcely look on't.
Such a foe, good heavens!   *Exit [into the cave].* 27
          Enter Belarius, Guiderius, and Arviragus.

BELARIUS
You, Polydore, have proved best woodman and   28
Are master of the feast. Cadwal and I
Will play the cook and servant; 'tis our match.   30
The sweat of industry would dry and die
But for the end it works to. Come, our stomachs
Will make what's homely savory. Weariness   33
Can snore upon the flint when resty sloth   34
Finds the down pillow hard. Now peace be here,
Poor house, that keep'st thyself.   36
GUIDERIUS   I am throughly weary.
ARVIRAGUS
I am weak with toil, yet strong in appetite.
GUIDERIUS
There is cold meat i' th' cave. We'll browse on that   38
Whilst what we have killed be cooked.
BELARIUS *[looking into the cave]*   Stay, come not in.
But that it eats our victuals, I should think
Here were a fairy.
GUIDERIUS   What's the matter, sir?

18 *hold* stronghold   **19** *were best* had better   **20** *clean* completely; *nature*
i.e. a person   **21** *hardness* hardship   **22** *hardiness* courage, endurance   **24**
Take or lend i.e. she expects the civil person to speak, the savage to act, be it
to take (life or money) or give (food or blows)   **27** *Such ... heavens*
heavens grant me such a foe   **28** *woodman* hunter   **30** *match* bargain   **33**
homely plain   **34** *resty* lazy   **36** *keep'st* takest care of; *throughly*
thoroughly   **38** *browse* nibble

BELARIUS
By Jupiter, an angel! or, if not,
An earthly paragon! Behold divineness
No elder than a boy!
          Enter Imogen.

IMOGEN
Good masters, harm me not.
Before I entered here, I called and thought
47 To have begged or bought what I have took. Good troth,
I have stol'n naught, nor would not, though I had found
Gold strewed i' th' floor. Here's money for my meat.
I would have left it on the board so soon
As I had made my meal, and parted
With pray'rs for the provider.

GUIDERIUS   Money, youth?

ARVIRAGUS
All gold and silver rather turn to dirt,
54 An 'tis no better reckoned but of those
Who worship dirty gods.

IMOGEN   I see you're angry.
Know, if you kill me for my fault, I should
Have died had I not made it.

BELARIUS   Whither bound?

IMOGEN
To Milford Haven.

BELARIUS
What's your name?

IMOGEN
Fidele, sir. I have a kinsman who
Is bound for Italy; he embarked at Milford;
62 To whom being going, almost spent with hunger,
63 I am fall'n in this offense.

BELARIUS   Prithee, fair youth,
Think us no churls, nor measure our good minds
By this rude place we live in. Well encountered!

47 *Good troth* in truth   54 *of* by   62 *spent* exhausted   63 *in* into

'Tis almost night; you shall have better cheer   66
Ere you depart, and thanks to stay and eat it.   67
Boys, bid him welcome.

GUIDERIUS   Were you a woman, youth,
I should woo hard but be your groom in honesty.   69
I bid for you as I do buy.   70

ARVIRAGUS   I'll make't my comfort
He is a man. I'll love him as my brother,
And such a welcome as I'ld give to him
After long absence, such is yours. Most welcome.
Be sprightly, for you fall 'mongst friends.   74

IMOGEN   'Mongst friends?
If brothers. *[aside]* Would it had been so that they
Had been my father's sons! Then had my prize   76
Been less, and so more equal ballasting   77
To thee, Posthumus.

BELARIUS   He wrings at some distress.   78

GUIDERIUS
Would I could free't!

ARVIRAGUS   Or I, whate'er it be,
What pain it cost, what danger. Gods!

BELARIUS   Hark, boys.
          [Whispers.]

IMOGEN
Great men
That had a court no bigger than this cave,
That did attend themselves and had the virtue   83
Which their own conscience sealed them, laying by   84
That nothing-gift of differing multitudes,   85
Could not outpeer these twain. Pardon me, gods,   86

---

66 *cheer* entertainment   67 *thanks to* i.e. we'll be pleased to have you   69 *but be* but to be   70 *I bid ... buy* (literal meaning not clear; the idea is that he sets a high value on Fidele, as in making a serious bid for purchase)   74 *sprightly* in good spirits   76 *prize* (pun on the meanings 'value' and 'captured ship')   77 *less* i.e. she would not have been heir to the throne; *ballasting* weight, position   78 *wrings* writhes   83 *attend* serve   84 *laying by* disregarding   85 *nothing-gift* worthless gift (admission? attendance?); *differing* inconsistent   86 *outpeer* excel

I'ld change my sex to be companion with them,
Since Leonatus' false.

BELARIUS   It shall be so.
89 Boys, we'll go dress our hunt. Fair youth, come in.
90 Discourse is heavy, fasting. When we have supped,
We'll mannerly demand thee of thy story,
So far as thou wilt speak it.

GUIDERIUS   Pray draw near.

ARVIRAGUS
The night to th' owl and morn to th' lark less welcome.

IMOGEN
Thanks, sir.

ARVIRAGUS
I pray draw near.   *Exeunt.*

*

III, vii   *Enter two Roman Senators, and Tribunes.*

I. SENATOR
1 This is the tenor of the Emperor's writ:
That since the common men are now in action
'Gainst the Pannonians and Dalmatians,
And that the legions now in Gallia are
5 Full weak to undertake our wars against
6 The fall'n-off Britons, that we do incite
The gentry to this business. He creates
Lucius proconsul, and to you the tribunes,
9 For this immediate levy, he commands
10 His absolute commission. Long live Caesar!

TRIBUNE
Is Lucius general of the forces?

2. SENATOR   Ay.

TRIBUNE
Remaining now in Gallia?

---

89 *dress our hunt* prepare our game   90 *Discourse . . . fasting* conservation is
burdensome when we have not eaten
III, vii Rome: Senate House   1 *writ* dispatch   5 *Full* quite   6 *fall'n-off*
revolted; *incite* summon   9 *commands* entrusts   10 *commission* authority

1. SENATOR   With those legions
Which I have spoke of, whereunto your levy
Must be supplyant. The words of your commission   14
Will tie you to the numbers and the time   15
Of their dispatch.
TRIBUNE   We will discharge our duty.   *Exeunt.*

*

Enter Cloten alone.   IV, i

CLOTEN I am near to th' place where they should meet, if
Pisanio have mapped it truly. How fit his garments serve 2
me! Why should his mistress, who was made by him
that made the tailor, not be fit too? The rather, saving 4
reverence of the word, for 'tis said a woman's fitness 5
comes by fits. Therein I must play the workman. I dare 6
speak it to myself, for it is not vainglory for a man and
his glass to confer in his own chamber – I mean, the lines 8
of my body are as well drawn as his; no less young, more
strong, not beneath him in fortunes, beyond him in the
advantage of the time, above him in birth, alike con- 11
versant in general services, and more remarkable in 12
single oppositions. Yet this imperceiverant thing loves 13
him in my despite. What mortality is! Posthumus, thy 14
head, which now is growing upon thy shoulders, shall
within this hour be off, thy mistress enforced, thy gar- 16
ments cut to pieces before thy face; and all this done, 17
spurn her home to her father, who may happily be a little 18
angry for my so rough usage; but my mother, having

14 *supplyant* supplementary   15 *tie you to* specify to you
IV, i Wales: before the cave of Belarius 2 *fit* fittingly 4 *fit* i.e. for me
(with pun on the meaning 'inclined to') 4–5 *saving reverence* with all due
respect to you (apology to audience for puns on *fit*) 5 *for* since; *fitness*
inclination (i.e. sexual) 6 *fits* (cf. 'fits and starts') 8 *glass* mirror 11 *of
the time* in the present (social) world; *alike conversant* equally experienced
12 *services* i.e. military 13 *oppositions* combats; *imperceiverant* unper-
ceiving 14 *What mortality is* what a thing life is 16 *enforced* raped 17
thy face (some editors emend 'thy' to 'her') 18 *spurn* kick; *happily* (as
elsewhere, for 'haply,' perchance)

20 power of his testiness, shall turn all into my commenda-
21 tions. My horse is tied up safe. Out, sword, and to a sore
22 purpose! Fortune put them into my hand. This is the
very description of their meeting place, and the fellow
dares not deceive me.   *Exit.*

IV, ii   *Enter Belarius, Guiderius, Arviragus, and Imogen
from the cave.*

BELARIUS *[to Imogen]*
You are not well. Remain here in the cave;
We'll come to you after hunting.

ARVIRAGUS *[to Imogen]*   Brother, stay here.
Are we not brothers?

IMOGEN   So man and man should be,
4   But clay and clay differs in dignity,
5   Whose dust is both alike. I am very sick.

GUIDERIUS
Go you to hunting; I'll abide with him.

IMOGEN
So sick I am not, yet I am not well,
8   But not so citizen a wanton as
To seem to die ere sick. So please you, leave me;
10 Stick to your journal course; the breach of custom
Is breach of all. I am ill, but your being by me
12 Cannot amend me; society is no comfort
To one not sociable. I am not very sick,
Since I can reason of it. Pray you trust me here—
I'll rob none but myself—and let me die,
16 Stealing so poorly.

GUIDERIUS   I love thee—I have spoke it—
17 How much the quantity, the weight as much
As I do love my father.

BELARIUS   What? How, how?

20 *power of* control over; *commendations* credit   21 *sore* causing pain   22
This is this place fits
IV, ii   4 *clay and clay* different persons   5 *dust* remains after death   8
citizen city-bred (cf. 'citified,' 'sissy'); *wanton* spoiled child   10 *journal*
daily, regular; *breach* disruption   12 *amend* make better   16 *poorly* i.e.
from myself only   17 *How . . . as much* as much, as deeply

ARVIRAGUS
    If it be sin to say so, sir, I yoke me   19
    In my good brother's fault. I know not why
    I love this youth, and I have heard you say
    Love's reason 's without reason. The bier at door,
    And a demand who is't shall die, I'ld say
    'My father, not this youth.'
BELARIUS [aside]   O noble strain!   24
    O worthiness of nature, breed of greatness!
    Cowards father cowards and base things sire base;   26
    Nature hath meal and bran, contempt and grace.   27
    I'm not their father; yet who this should be   28
    Doth miracle itself, loved before me. –
    'Tis the ninth hour o' th' morn.
ARVIRAGUS   Brother, farewell.
IMOGEN
    I wish ye sport.
ARVIRAGUS   You health.
        [To Belarius]   So please you, sir.   31
IMOGEN [aside]
    These are kind creatures. Gods, what lies I have heard!
    Our courtiers say all 's savage but at court.
    Experience, O, thou disprov'st report!
    Th' imperious seas breeds monsters; for the dish   35
    Poor tributary rivers as sweet fish.   36
    I am sick still, heartsick. Pisanio,
    I'll now taste of thy drug.
        [Swallows some.]
GUIDERIUS   I could not stir him.   38
    He said he was gentle, but unfortunate;   39
    Dishonestly afflicted, but yet honest.

19–20 *yoke ... fault* confess to having committed the same fault as my brother 24 *strain* lineage, heredity 26, 27 (in the folio text, these lines are introduced by quotation marks to identify them as maxims or well-known sayings) 28–29 *who ... me* that this person, whoever he may be, should be loved ahead of me is miraculous 31 *So please you* at your command 35 *imperious* imperial 36 *rivers ... fish* rivers (breed) just as sweet fish (as the sea does) 38 *stir* move (to tell about himself) 39 *gentle* of noble birth

ARVIRAGUS
Thus did he answer me, yet said hereafter
I might know more.
BELARIUS   To th' field, to th' field.
[To Imogen]
We'll leave you for this time; go in and rest.
ARVIRAGUS
We'll not be long away.
BELARIUS   Pray be not sick,
For you must be our housewife.
IMOGEN   Well or ill,
46   I am bound to you.   *Exit [into the cave].*
BELARIUS   And shalt be ever.
This youth, howe'er distressed, appears he hath had
Good ancestors.
ARVIRAGUS   How angel-like he sings!
GUIDERIUS
49   But his neat cookery! He cut our roots in characters,
50   And sauced our broths as Juno had been sick
51   And he her dieter.
ARVIRAGUS   Nobly he yokes
A smiling with a sigh, as if the sigh
53   Was that it was for not being such a smile;
The smile mocking the sigh that it would fly
From so divine a temple to commix
With winds that sailors rail at.
GUIDERIUS   I do note
57   That grief and patience, rooted in them both,
58   Mingle their spurs together.
ARVIRAGUS   Grow patience,
59   And let the stinking elder, grief, untwine
60   His perishing root with the increasing vine.

46 *bound* obligated; *shalt be* i.e. bound (by emotional ties) 49 *neat* fine,
elegant; *characters* letters (of the alphabet), designs 50 *as* as if 51 *dieter*
dietitian 53 *that* what 57 *them* i.e. the smile and sigh (some editors
emend to 'him') 58 *spurs* roots 59 *elder* elder tree 60 *perishing*
noxious; *with . . . vine* from the increasing vine (?), as the vine increases (?)

BELARIUS
It is great morning. Come away. Who's there?   61
   Enter Cloten.

CLOTEN
I cannot find those runagates. That villain   62
Hath mocked me. I am faint.   63

BELARIUS   'Those runagates'?
Means he not us? I partly know him. 'Tis
Cloten, the son o' th' Queen. I fear some ambush.
I saw him not these many years, and yet
I know 'tis he. We are held as outlaws. Hence!   67

GUIDERIUS
He is but one. You and my brother search
What companies are near. Pray you, away.   69
Let me alone with him. *[Exeunt Belarius and Arviragus.]*

CLOTEN   Soft, what are you   70
That fly me thus? Some villain mountaineers?
I have heard of such. What slave art thou?

GUIDERIUS   A thing
More slavish did I ne'er than answering
A 'slave' without a knock.   74

CLOTEN   Thou art a robber,
A lawbreaker, a villain. Yield thee, thief.

GUIDERIUS
To who? To thee? What art thou? Have not I
An arm as big as thine? A heart as big?
Thy words, I grant, are bigger, for I wear not
My dagger in my mouth. Say what thou art,
Why I should yield to thee.

CLOTEN   Thou villain base,
Know'st me not by my clothes?   81

GUIDERIUS   No, nor thy tailor, rascal,

---

61 *great morning* broad daylight 62 *runagates* runaways 63 *mocked* fooled 67 *held* regarded 69 *companies* followers 70 *Soft* stop (exclamation; cf. 'take it easy') 74 *'slave'* (Guiderius may be quoting Cloten's word or simply calling Cloten a slave) 81 *clothes* i.e. court clothes

    Who is thy grandfather. He made those clothes,
    Which, as it seems, make thee.

83 CLOTEN   Thou precious varlet,
    My tailor made them not.

    GUIDERIUS   Hence then, and thank
    The man that gave them thee. Thou art some fool;
    I am loath to beat thee.

86 CLOTEN   Thou injurious thief,
    Hear but my name and tremble.

    GUIDERIUS   What's thy name?

    CLOTEN
    Cloten, thou villain.

    GUIDERIUS
    Cloten, thou double villain, be thy name,
    I cannot tremble at it. Were it Toad, or Adder, Spider,
    'Twould move me sooner.

    CLOTEN   To thy further fear,
92 Nay, to thy mere confusion, thou shalt know
    I am son to th' Queen.

93 GUIDERIUS   I am sorry for't; not seeming
    So worthy as thy birth.

    CLOTEN   Art not afeard?

    GUIDERIUS
    Those that I reverence, those I fear – the wise;
    At fools I laugh, not fear them.

96 CLOTEN   Die the death!
97 When I have slain thee with my proper hand,
    I'll follow those that even now fled hence
    And on the gates of Lud's town set your heads.
    Yield, rustic mountaineer.   *Fight and exeunt.*
       Enter Belarius and Arviragus.

    BELARIUS
101 No company's abroad?

83 *varlet* knave 86 *injurious* insulting 92 *mere confusion* utter destruction
93 *not seeming* since you do not seem 96 *Die the death* (as if he were
imposing a legal sentence) 97 *proper* own 101 *abroad* around, in the
neighborhood

ARVIRAGUS
　None in the world. You did mistake him sure.

BELARIUS
　I cannot tell. Long is it since I saw him,
　But time hath nothing blurred those lines of favor　104
　Which then he wore. The snatches in his voice,　105
　And burst of speaking, were as his. I am absolute　106
　'Twas very Cloten.　107

ARVIRAGUS　　　In this place we left them.
　I wish my brother make good time with him,　108
　You say he is so fell.　109

BELARIUS　　　Being scarce made up,
　I mean to man, he had not apprehension　110
　Of roaring terrors; for defect of judgment　111
　Is oft the cause of fear.

Enter Guiderius [with Cloten's head].
　　　　　　　　　But see, thy brother.

GUIDERIUS
　This Cloten was a fool, an empty purse;
　There was no money in't. Not Hercules
　Could have knocked out his brains, for he had none.
　Yet I not doing this, the fool had borne
　My head as I do his.

BELARIUS　　　What hast thou done?
　I am perfect what: cut off one Cloten's head,　118
　Son to the Queen, after his own report;
　Who called me traitor, mountaineer, and swore

---

104 *lines of favor* facial lines　105 *snatches* catches, hesitations　106 *absolute* positive　107 *very Cloten* Cloten himself　108 *make good time* may succeed (cf. 'have a good day')　109 *fell* savage; *made up* grown up (in sense of years or mental ability)　110 *apprehension* understanding 111–12 *defect ... fear* (1) some editors think that there is a scribal or typographic error, such as *cause* for 'cease'; (2) other editors, that Shakespeare wrote these words but was careless about meaning; (3) others, that Shakespeare wrote the words and intended this meaning: Cloten was fearless because he had no wits at all instead of some wits defectively used (*defect of judgment*)　118 *perfect* aware

121 With his own single hand he'ld take us in,
Displace our heads where – thank the gods – they grow,
And set them on Lud's town.

BELARIUS   We are all undone.

GUIDERIUS
Why, worthy father, what have we to lose
125 But that he swore to take, our lives? The law
126 Protects not us. Then why should we be tender
To let an arrogant piece of flesh threat us,
Play judge and executioner all himself,
129 For we do fear the law? What company
Discover you abroad?

BELARIUS   No single soul
Can we set eye on, but in all safe reason
132 He must have some attendants. Though his honor
Was nothing but mutation – ay, and that
From one bad thing to worse – not frenzy, not
Absolute madness could so far have raved
To bring him here alone. Although perhaps
It may be heard at court that such as we
Cave here, hunt here, are outlaws, and in time
139 May make some stronger head; the which he hearing –
As it is like him – might break out, and swear
141 He'ld fetch us in; yet is't not probable
142 To come alone, either he so undertaking,
143 Or they so suffering. Then on good ground we fear,
144 If we do fear this body hath a tail
More perilous than the head.

145 ARVIRAGUS   Let ordinance
Come as the gods foresay it. Howsoe'er,
My brother hath done well.

---

121 *take us in* subdue us   125 *that* what   126–27 *tender To* so tolerant as to   129 *For* because   132 *honor* (implies steadfastness; ironically joined with *mutation*, changeableness. Some editors emend to 'humor')   139 *make . . . head* become a stronger force   141 *fetch us in* capture us   142 *To come* for him to come   143 *suffering* permitting (it)   144 *tail* i.e. what comes after: followers hostile to us   145 *ordinance* whatever is ordained

BELARIUS   I had no mind
To hunt this day. The boy Fidele's sickness
Did make my way long forth.   149

GUIDERIUS   With his own sword,
Which he did wave against my throat, I have ta'en
His head from him. I'll throw't into the creek
Behind our rock, and let it to the sea
And tell the fishes he's the Queen's son, Cloten.
That's all I reck.   *Exit.* 154

BELARIUS   I fear 'twill be revenged.
Would, Polydore, thou hadst not done't, though valor
Becomes thee well enough.

ARVIRAGUS   Would I had done't,
So the revenge alone pursued me. Polydore,   157
I love thee brotherly, but envy much
Thou hast robbed me of this deed. I would revenges
That possible strength might meet would seek us through 160
And put us to our answer.   161

BELARIUS   Well, 'tis done.
We'll hunt no more to-day, nor seek for danger
Where there's no profit. I prithee, to our rock;
You and Fidele play the cooks. I'll stay
Till hasty Polydore return, and bring him   165
To dinner presently.

ARVIRAGUS   Poor sick Fidele,
I'll willingly to him. To gain his color   167
I'ld let a parish of such Clotens blood   168
And praise myself for charity.   *Exit.*

BELARIUS   O thou goddess,
Thou divine Nature, thou thyself thou blazon'st   170
In these two princely boys! They are as gentle
As zephyrs blowing below the violet,

149 *Did . . . forth* made my walk forth (from the cave) seem long 154 *reck*
care 157 *So* so that; *pursued* would have pursued 160 *possible* our
available; *meet* i.e. in combat; *seek us through* come upon us 161 *put*
force 165 *hasty* quick to act 167 *gain his color* restore the color (to) his
(cheeks) 168 *let . . . blood* let blood for a parish of such Clotens (a medical
term as a metaphor for 'kill') 170 *blazon'st* depictest

Not wagging his sweet head ; and yet as rough,
174 Their royal blood enchafed, as the rud'st wind
That by the top doth take the mountain pine
And make him stoop to th' vale. 'Tis wonder
177 That an invisible instinct should frame them
178 To royalty unlearned, honor untaught,
179 Civility not seen from other, valor
180 That wildly grows in them but yields a crop
As if it had been sowed. Yet still it's strange
What Cloten's being here to us portends,
Or what his death will bring us.
          Enter Guiderius.
GUIDERIUS   Where's my brother ?
184 I have sent Cloten's clotpoll down the stream
In embassy to his mother ; his body's hostage
For his return.
          Solemn music.
186 BELARIUS   My ingenious instrument !
Hark, Polydore, it sounds. But what occasion
188 Hath Cadwal now to give it motion ? Hark !
GUIDERIUS
Is he at home ?
189 BELARIUS   He went hence even now.
GUIDERIUS
What does he mean ? Since death of my dear'st mother
It did not speak before. All solemn things
192 Should answer solemn accidents. The matter ?
193 Triumphs for nothing and lamenting toys
Is jollity for apes and grief for boys.
Is Cadwal mad ?
          *Enter Arviragus, with Imogen dead, bearing her in
          his arms.*

174 *enchafed* heated   177 *frame* direct   178 *royalty* kingly conduct   179
Civility civilized conduct   180 *wildly* spontaneously   184 *clotpoll* block-
head   186 *ingenious* skillfully constructed   188 *give it motion* play it   189
even just   192 *answer* correspond to; *accidents* events   193 *lamenting toys*
lamenting for trifles

BELARIUS　　　　Look, here he comes,
And brings the dire occasion in his arms
Of what we blame him for.

ARVIRAGUS　　　　　　The bird is dead
That we have made so much on. I had rather　　198
Have skipped from sixteen years of age to sixty,
To have turned my leaping time into a crutch,
Than have seen this.

GUIDERIUS　　　　　O sweetest, fairest lily!
My brother wears thee not the one half so well
As when thou grew'st thyself.

BELARIUS　　　　　　　O melancholy,
Who ever yet could sound thy bottom, find　　204
The ooze, to show what coast thy sluggish crare　　205
Might eas'liest harbor in? Thou blessèd thing,　　206
Jove knows what man thou mightst have made; but I,　　207
Thou diedst, a most rare boy, of melancholy.
How found you him?

ARVIRAGUS　　　　　Stark, as you see,　　209
Thus smiling, as some fly had tickled slumber,　　210
Not as death's dart being laughed at; his right cheek　　211
Reposing on a cushion.

GUIDERIUS　　　　　Where?

ARVIRAGUS　　　　　　O' th' floor;
His arms thus leagued. I thought he slept, and put　　213
My clouted brogues from off my feet, whose rudeness　　214
Answered my steps too loud.

GUIDERIUS　　　　　Why, he but sleeps.
If he be gone, he'll make his grave a bed;
With female fairies will his tomb be haunted,
And worms will not come to thee.

ARVIRAGUS　　　　　　　With fairest flowers,

---

198 *on* of　**204** *sound thy bottom* measure thy depths　**205** *crare* small boat
206 *thing* i.e. Fidele　**207** *but I* but I know that　**209** *Stark* stiff (in rigor
mortis)　**210** *as* as if　**211** *as ... at* as if the sting of death were being
laughed at　**213** *leagued* crossed　**214** *clouted brogues* nail-studded boots;
rudeness coarseness (of the boots)

Whilst summer lasts and I live here, Fidele,
I'll sweeten thy sad grave. Thou shalt not lack
The flower that's like thy face, pale primrose; nor
222   The azured harebell, like thy veins; no, nor
The leaf of eglantine, whom not to slander,
224   Outsweet'ned not thy breath. The ruddock would
With charitable bill – O bill, sore shaming
Those rich-left heirs that let their fathers lie
Without a monument! – bring thee all this,
Yea, and furred moss besides. When flowers are none
229   To winter-ground thy corse –

GUIDERIUS   Prithee have done,
230   And do not play in wench-like words with that
Which is so serious. Let us bury him,
And not protract with admiration what
Is now due debt. To th' grave.

233 ARVIRAGUS   Say, where shall's lay him?

GUIDERIUS
By good Euriphile, our mother.

ARVIRAGUS   Be't so.
And let us, Polydore, though now our voices
236   Have got the mannish crack, sing him to th' ground,
As once to our mother; use like note and words,
Save that Euriphile must be Fidele.

GUIDERIUS
Cadwal,
240   I cannot sing. I'll weep, and word it with thee,
For notes of sorrow out of tune are worse
242   Than priests and fanes that lie.

ARVIRAGUS   We'll speak it then.

BELARIUS
Great griefs, I see, med'cine the less, for Cloten

---

222 *azured* sky-blue   224 *ruddock* robin   229 *To winter-ground* to protect
in winter (?) (or it may be a prepositional phrase belonging to uncompleted
predicate of interrupted sentence)   230 *wench-like* womanish   233 *shall's*
shall us (we)   236 *crack* break, tone   240 *word* speak, recite   242 *fanes*
temples

Is quite forgot. He was a queen's son, boys,
And though he came our enemy, remember
He was paid for that. Though mean and mighty, rotting   246
Together, have one dust, yet reverence,
That angel of the world, doth make distinction   248
Of place 'tween high and low. Our foe was princely,
And though you took his life as being our foe,   250
Yet bury him as a prince.

GUIDERIUS   Pray you fetch him hither.
Thersites' body is as good as Ajax'   252
When neither are alive.

ARVIRAGUS   If you'll go fetch him,
We'll say our song the whilst. Brother, begin.

                        [Exit Belarius.]

GUIDERIUS
Nay, Cadwal, we must lay his head to th' east;   255
My father hath a reason for't.

ARVIRAGUS   'Tis true.

GUIDERIUS
Come on then and remove him.

ARVIRAGUS   So. Begin.

Song.

GUIDERIUS   Fear no more the heat o' th' sun
                    Nor the furious winter's rages;
              Thou thy worldly task hast done,
                    Home art gone and ta'en thy wages.
              Golden lads and girls all must,   262
              As chimney-sweepers, come to dust.   263

ARVIRAGUS   Fear no more the frown o' th' great;
              Thou art past the tyrant's stroke.

---

246 *paid* punished   248 *angel ... world* messenger sent from heaven to earth   250 *as being* because he was   252 *Thersites* vindictive and foul-mouthed Greek; *Ajax* Greek hero   255 *to th'east* (the opposite of Christian practice; a way of suggesting the non-Christian world of the play)   262 *Golden* i.e. fine   263 *As* like

                       Care no more to clothe and eat;
                         To thee the reed is as the oak.
268   The sceptre, learning, physic, must
                       All follow this and come to dust.

GUIDERIUS   Fear no more the lightning flash,
271 ARVIRAGUS   Nor th' all-dreaded thunder-stone;
GUIDERIUS   Fear no slander, censure rash;
ARVIRAGUS   Thou hast finished joy and moan.
BOTH   All lovers young, all lovers must
275   Consign to thee and come to dust.

276 GUIDERIUS   No exorciser harm thee,
ARVIRAGUS   Nor no witchcraft charm thee.
278 GUIDERIUS   Ghost unlaid forbear thee;
ARVIRAGUS   Nothing ill come near thee.
280 BOTH   Quiet consummation have,
                       And renownèd be thy grave.

Enter Belarius with the body of Cloten.

GUIDERIUS
We have done our obsequies. Come, lay him down.
BELARIUS
Here's a few flowers, but 'bout midnight, more.
The herbs that have on them cold dew o' th' night
285 Are strewings fitt'st for graves. Upon their faces.
286 You were as flow'rs, now withered; even so
287 These herblets shall which we upon you strew.
Come on, away; apart upon our knees.
The ground that gave them first has them again.
Their pleasures here are past, so is their pain.
          Exeunt [Belarius, Guiderius, and Arviragus].
      Imogen awakes.

268 *sceptre, learning, physic* kings, scholars, doctors   271 *thunder-stone* thunderbolt   275 *Consign* perhaps, co-sign (i.e. the same contract: meet the same fate)   276 *exorciser* conjurer   278 *unlaid* not driven out (by formal procedures); *forbear* leave alone   280 *consummation* fulfillment (i.e. death)   285 *Upon their faces* flowers on front of bodies (?), flowers lying face down (?)   286 *now* now you are   287 *shall* shall be (withered)

[IMOGEN]
 Yes, sir, to Milford Haven. Which is the way?
 I thank you. By yond bush? Pray, how far thither?
 'Ods pittikins, can it be six mile yet?   293
 I have gone all night. Faith, I'll lie down and sleep. 294
  [Sees the body of Cloten.]
 But, soft, no bedfellow! O gods and goddesses!
 These flow'rs are like the pleasures of the world;
 This bloody man, the care on't. I hope I dream,
 For so I thought I was a cave-keeper   298
 And cook to honest creatures. But 'tis not so;
 'Twas but a bolt of nothing, shot at nothing, 300
 Which the brain makes of fumes. Our very eyes 301
 Are sometimes like our judgments, blind. Good faith,
 I tremble still with fear, but if there be
 Yet left in heaven as small a drop of pity
 As a wren's eye, feared gods, a part of it!   305
 The dream's here still. Even when I wake it is
 Without me, as within me; not imagined, felt.
 A headless man? The garments of Posthumus?
 I know the shape of's leg; this is his hand,
 His foot Mercurial, his Martial thigh,   310
 The brawns of Hercules; but his Jovial face – 311
 Murder in heaven? How? 'Tis gone. Pisanio,
 All curses madded Hecuba gave the Greeks, 313
 And mine to boot, be darted on thee! Thou,
 Conspired with that irregulous devil Cloten, 315
 Hath here cut off my lord. To write and read
 Be henceforth treacherous! Damned Pisanio
 Hath with his forgèd letters – damned Pisanio –

---

293 *'Ods pittikins* God's little pity (diminutive of '[I pray for] God's pity';
cf. ll. 304–05) **294** *gone* walked **298** *so* i.e. in a dream (such as this may
be); *cave-keeper* cave dweller **300** *bolt* arrow **301** *fumes* vapors believed
to rise from the body to the brain and cause dreams **305** *a part* i.e. grant
me a part **310** *Mercurial* quick, like Mercury's; *Martial* powerful, like
Mars' **311** *brawns* muscles; *Jovial* like that of Jove, king of the gods **313**
madded maddened; *Hecuba* wife of Priam, king of Troy, destroyed by the
Greeks **315** *Conspired* conspiring; *irregulous* lawless

From this most bravest vessel of the world
Struck the maintop. O Posthumus, alas,
Where is thy head? Where's that? Ay me, where's that?
Pisanio might have killed thee at the heart
And left this head on. How should this be? Pisanio?
324 'Tis he and Cloten. Malice and lucre in them
325 Have laid this woe here. O, 'tis pregnant, pregnant!
The drug he gave me, which he said was precious
327 And cordial to me, have I not found it
328 Murd'rous to th' senses? That confirms it home.
329 This is Pisanio's deed, and Cloten. O,
Give color to my pale cheek with thy blood,
That we the horrider may seem to those
332 Which chance to find us. O my lord, my lord!
    [Falls on the body.]
    Enter Lucius, Captains, and a Soothsayer.

CAPTAIN
333 To them the legions garrisoned in Gallia
334 After your will have crossed the sea, attending
    You here at Milford Haven with your ships.
    They are here in readiness.

LUCIUS   But what from Rome?

CAPTAIN
337 The Senate hath stirred up the confiners
    And gentlemen of Italy, most willing spirits
    That promise noble service, and they come
    Under the conduct of bold Iachimo,
341 Siena's brother.

LUCIUS   When expect you them?

CAPTAIN
With the next benefit o' th' wind.

342 LUCIUS   This forwardness

324 *lucre* greed   325 *pregnant* clear   327 *cordial* of medicinal value   328 *home* entirely (cf. 'drives the point home')   329 *Cloten* (idiomatic for 'Cloten's')   332 *Which* who   333 *To* besides; *them* i.e. forces mentioned by officers before coming on stage   334 *After* according to; *attending* waiting for   337 *confiners* inhabitants   341 *Siena's* lord of Siena's   342 *forwardness* moving ahead (on schedule)

Makes our hopes fair. Command our present numbers   343
Be mustered; bid the captains look to't. Now, sir,
What have you dreamed of late of this war's purpose?   345

SOOTHSAYER

Last night the very gods showed me a vision –
I fast and prayed for their intelligence – thus: 347
I saw Jove's bird, the Roman eagle, winged
From the spongy south to this part of the west,   349
There vanished in the sunbeams; which portends,
Unless my sins abuse my divination,   351
Success to th' Roman host.

LUCIUS   Dream often so,
And never false. Soft, ho, what trunk is here?   353
Without his top? The ruin speaks that sometime
It was a worthy building. How, a page?
Or dead or sleeping on him? But dead rather,   356
For nature doth abhor to make his bed   357
With the defunct or sleep upon the dead.   358
Let's see the boy's face.

CAPTAIN   He's alive, my lord.

LUCIUS

He'll, then, instruct us of this body. Young one,   360
Inform us of thy fortunes, for it seems
They crave to be demanded. Who is this   362
Thou mak'st thy bloody pillow? Or who was he
That, otherwise than noble nature did,   364
Hath altered that good picture? What's thy interest
In this sad wrack? How came't? Who is't? What art   366
thou?

IMOGEN

I am nothing, or if not,

343 *fair* strong   345 *of late* lately; *this war's purpose* our achieving our
purpose in this war   347 *fast* fasted; *their intelligence* information from
them   349 *spongy* damp   351 *abuse* mislead   353 *false* (dream) falsely
356 *Or* either   357 *nature doth abhor* man naturally abhors   358 *defunct*
dead   360 *instruct us of* inform us about   362 *crave ... demanded* beg to
be asked about (i.e. are such as to arouse curiosity or sympathy)   364
otherwise ... did from the form given it by noble nature   366 *wrack* ruin

Nothing to be were better. This was my master,
A very valiant Briton and a good,
That here by mountaineers lies slain. Alas,
There is no more such masters. I may wander
From east to occident, cry out for service,
Try many, all good, serve truly, never
Find such another master.

LUCIUS   'Lack, good youth

375 Thou mov'st no less with thy complaining than
Thy master in bleeding. Say his name, good friend.

IMOGEN

Richard du Champ. *[aside]* If I do lie and do
No harm by it, though the gods hear, I hope
They'll pardon it. Say you, sir ?

LUCIUS   Thy name ?

IMOGEN   Fidele, sir.

LUCIUS

380 Thou dost approve thyself the very same ;
Thy name well fits thy faith, thy faith thy name.
Wilt take thy chance with me ? I will not say
Thou shalt be so well mastered, but be sure
No less beloved. The Roman emperor's letters
Sent by a consul to me should not sooner

386 Than thine own worth prefer thee. Go with me.

IMOGEN

I'll follow, sir. But first, an't please the gods,
I'll hide my master from the flies, as deep

389 As these poor pickaxes can dig ; and when
With wild wood-leaves and weeds I ha' strewed his grave

391 And on it said a century of prayers,

392 Such as I can, twice o'er, I'll weep and sigh,
And leaving so his service, follow you,

394 So please you entertain me.

LUCIUS   Ay, good youth,

375 *mov'st no less* art no less moving   380 *approve* prove   386 *prefer*
recommend   389 *pickaxes* i.e. fingers   391 *century* hundred   392 *can*
know   394 *So* if it; *entertain* employ

And rather father thee than master thee.
My friends,
The boy hath taught us manly duties. Let us
Find out the prettiest daisied plot we can
And make him with our pikes and partisans   399
A grave. Come, arm him. Boy, he's preferred   400
By thee to us, and he shall be interred
As soldiers can. Be cheerful ; wipe thine eyes.
Some falls are means the happier to arise.   *Exeunt.*

*

Enter Cymbeline, Lords, and Pisanio.   IV, iii
CYMBELINE
Again, and bring me word how 'tis with her.
                        [Exit an Attendant.]
A fever with the absence of her son,
A madness, of which her life's in danger. Heavens,
How deeply you at once do touch me ! Imogen,   4
The great part of my comfort, gone ; my queen
Upon a desperate bed, and in a time   6
When fearful wars point at me ; her son gone,
So needful for this present. It strikes me past   8
The hope of comfort. But for thee, fellow,
Who needs must know of her departure and
Dost seem so ignorant, we'll enforce it from thee   11
By a sharp torture.
PISANIO   Sir, my life is yours,
I humbly set it at your will ; but for my mistress,
I nothing know where she remains, why gone,
Nor when she purposes return. Beseech your Highness,
Hold me your loyal servant.   16

399 *partisans* long-handled weapons   400 *arm him* carry him in your
arms; *preferred* recommended
IV, iii A chamber in the palace   4 *touch* wound   6 *desperate* i.e. she is
critically ill   8 *needful* needed; *It ... past* the blow to me is beyond   11
enforce ... thee force you to talk, get it out of you   16 *Hold* consider

LORD   Good my liege,
The day that she was missing he was here.
I dare be bound he's true and shall perform
19 All parts of his subjection loyally. For Cloten,
There wants no diligence in seeking him,
21 And will no doubt be found.
CYMBELINE   The time is troublesome.
        [To Pisanio]
22 We'll slip you for a season, but our jealousy
23 Does yet depend.
LORD   So please your Majesty,
The Roman legions, all from Gallia drawn,
Are landed on your coast, with a supply
Of Roman gentlemen by the senate sent.
CYMBELINE
27 Now for the counsel of my son and queen!
28 I am amazed with matter.
LORD   Good my liege,
29 Your preparation can affront no less
30 Than what you hear of. Come more, for more you're
        ready.
31 The want is but to put those pow'rs in motion
That long to move.
CYMBELINE   I thank you. Let's withdraw,
And meet the time as it seeks us. We fear not
34 What can from Italy annoy us, but
We grieve at chances here. Away. *Exeunt [all but Pisanio].*
PISANIO
36 I heard no letter from my master since
I wrote him Imogen was slain. 'Tis strange.
Nor hear I from my mistress, who did promise

19 *subjection* duties as a subject   21 *will* he will; *troublesome* full of
troubles, seriously disturbed   22 *slip* turn loose; *jealousy* suspicion   23
depend hang (over you)   27 *Now for* if only I now had   28 *amazed with
matter* confused by (all the) business   29 *preparation* armed force; *affront*
confront   29–30 *no less Than* an army as large as   30 *Come more* if more
come   31 *The ... but* all that's needed is   34 *annoy* injure   36 *no letter*
not a whit

To yield me often tidings. Neither know I
What is betid to Cloten, but remain   40
Perplexed in all. The heavens still must work.
Wherein I am false I am honest; not true, to be true.
These present wars shall find I love my country,
Even to the note o' th' King, or I'll fall in them.   44
All other doubts, by time let them be cleared;
Fortune brings in some boats that are not steered.   *Exit.*

*

Enter Belarius, Guiderius, and Arviragus.   IV, iv
GUIDERIUS
  The noise is round about us.
BELARIUS   Let us from it.
ARVIRAGUS
  What pleasure, sir, find we in life, to lock it   2
  From action and adventure?
GUIDERIUS   Nay, what hope
  Have we in hiding us? This way the Romans   4
  Must or for Britons slay us or receive us   5
  For barbarous and unnatural revolts
  During their use, and slay us after.
BELARIUS   Sons,
  We'll higher to the mountains, there secure us.   8
  To the King's party there's no going. Newness   9
  Of Cloten's death – we being not known, not mustered   10
  Among the bands – may drive us to a render   11
  Where we have lived, and so extort from's that
  Which we have done, whose answer would be death   13
  Drawn on with torture.   14

40 *betid* happened   44 *note o'* recognition by
IV, iv Wales: before the cave of Belarius   2 *to lock it* when it is closed off
4 *This way* i.e. if we hide   5 *Must or* must either   5–7 *receive ... use*
i.e.accept us and use us for a time against the British, service which for us
would be barbarous and unnatural   8 *secure us* make ourselves safe   9
Newness recency   10 *mustered* enrolled   11 *render* account   13 *whose
answer* to which the reply (i.e. the penalty)   14 *Drawn on with* led up to by

GUIDERIUS   This is, sir, a doubt
In such a time nothing becoming you
Nor satisfying us.

ARVIRAGUS   It is not likely
That when they hear the Roman horses neigh,
18   Behold their quartered fires, have both their eyes
19   And ears so cloyed importantly as now,
20   That they will waste their time upon our note,
To know from whence we are.

BELARIUS   O, I am known
Of many in the army. Many years,
23   Though Cloten then but young, you see, not wore him
From my remembrance. And besides, the King
25   Hath not deserved my service nor your loves,
Who find in my exile the want of breeding,
27   The certainty of this hard life ; aye hopeless
28   To have the courtesy your cradle promised,
29   But to be still hot summer's tanlings and
The shrinking slaves of winter.

GUIDERIUS   Than be so
Better to cease to be. Pray, sir, to th' army.
I and my brother are not known ; yourself
33   So out of thought, and thereto so o'ergrown,
34   Cannot be questioned.

ARVIRAGUS   By this sun that shines,
I'll thither. What thing is't that I never
Did see man die, scarce ever looked on blood
37   But that of coward hares, hot goats, and venison !
Never bestrid a horse, save one that had

---

18 *quartered* camp **19** *cloyed importantly* filled with important business
20 *upon our note* in noticing us **23** *then* was then; *not wore* did not wear
(i.e. erase) **25–26** *your . . . breeding* the love of you two who because of my
exile meet with lack of cultivation **27** *certainty* inescapability **27–28**
hopeless . . . courtesy without hope of having the courtly style **28** *cradle*
birth **29** *tanlings* tanned persons, i.e. living in the open, unsheltered **33**
o'ergrown bearded (?), replaced (in their thoughts) (?) **34** *questioned* i.e. on
your identity **37** *hot* lecherous

A rider like myself, who ne'er wore rowel   39
Nor iron on his heel! I am ashamed
To look upon the holy sun, to have
The benefit of his blest beams, remaining
So long a poor unknown.
GUIDERIUS   By heavens, I'll go.
If you will bless me, sir, and give me leave,
I'll take the better care, but if you will not,
The hazard therefore due fall on me by   46
The hands of Romans!
ARVIRAGUS   So say I. Amen.
BELARIUS
No reason I, since of your lives you set   48
So slight a valuation, should reserve
My cracked one to more care. Have with you, boys!   50
If in your country wars you chance to die,   51
That is my bed too, lads, and there I'll lie.
Lead, lead. *[aside]* The time seems long; their blood
    thinks scorn
Till it fly out and show them princes born.   *Exeunt.*

*

Enter Posthumus alone [with a bloody handkerchief].   V, i
POSTHUMUS
Yea, bloody cloth, I'll keep thee, for I wished
Thou shouldst be colored thus. You married ones,
If each of you should take this course, how many   3
Must murder wives much better than themselves
For wrying but a little! O Pisanio,   5
Every good servant does not all commands;   6

39–40 *ne'er ... heel* i.e. never had standard riding equipment   46 *hazard
... due* danger arising from being unblessed   48 *of* on   50 *cracked* i.e.
with age   51 *country* country's
V, i An open place in Britain   3 *take this course* do as I have done   5
wrying erring   6 *does not* does not carry out

7 No bond but to do just ones. Gods, if you
   Should have ta'en vengeance on my faults, I never
9 Had lived to put on this ; so had you saved
10 The noble Imogen to repent, and struck
   Me, wretch more worth your vengeance. But alack,
   You snatch some hence for little faults ; that's love,
13 To have them fall no more ; you some permit
14 To second ills with ills, each elder worse,
15 And make them dread it, to the doers' thrift.
   But Imogen is your own. Do your best wills,
   And make me blessed to obey. I am brought hither
   Among th' Italian gentry, and to fight
   Against my lady's kingdom. 'Tis enough
   That, Britain, I have killed thy mistress ; peace,
   I'll give no wound to thee. Therefore, good heavens,
   Hear patiently my purpose. I'll disrobe me
23 Of these Italian weeds and suit myself
   As does a Briton peasant. So I'll fight
25 Against the part I come with ; so I'll die
   For thee, O Imogen, even for whom my life
   Is every breath a death ; and thus, unknown,
   Pitied nor hated, to the face of peril
   Myself I'll dedicate. Let me make men know
30 More valor in me than my habits show.
   Gods, put the strength o' th' Leonati in me.
32 To shame the guise o' th' world, I will begin
33 The fashion, less without and more within.

                                        Exit.

7 *No bond but* he is bound only   9 *put on* instigate (?), load myself with
(?)   10 *repent* i.e. for the misdeeds he imputes to her   13 *fall* i.e. into
misconduct   14 *second* duplicate, back up; *elder* i.e. later (as if evils were
becoming more 'mature' with time)   15 *them* i.e. the doers; *dread it* repent
the evil course; *thrift* profit, gain   23 *weeds* clothes; *suit* dress   25 *part*
side   30 *habits show* clothes proclaim   32 *guise* practice   33 *fashion, less
without* i.e. fashion of having less external show

Enter Lucius, Iachimo, and the Roman Army at   V, ii
one door, and the Briton Army at another, Leonatus
Posthumus following like a poor soldier. They march
over and go out. Then enter again in skirmish
Iachimo and Posthumus. He vanquisheth and
disarmeth Iachimo and then leaves him.

IACHIMO
The heaviness and guilt within my bosom
Takes off my manhood. I have belied a lady,   2
The princess of this country, and the air on't   3
Revengingly enfeebles me ; or could this carl,   4
A very drudge of nature's, have subdued me
In my profession ? Knighthoods and honors, borne
As I wear mine, are titles but of scorn.
If that thy gentry, Britain, go before   8
This lout as he exceeds our lords, the odds
Is that we scarce are men and you are gods.   *Exit.*
    The battle continues. The Britons fly ; Cymbeline is taken.
    Then enter, to his rescue, Belarius, Guiderius, and Arviragus.

BELARIUS
Stand, stand ! We have th' advantage of the ground.
The lane is guarded. Nothing routs us but
The villainy of our fears.
GUIDERIUS, ARVIRAGUS   Stand, stand, and fight !
    Enter Posthumus, and seconds the Britons. They
    rescue Cymbeline and exeunt. Then enter Lucius,
    Iachimo, and Imogen.

LUCIUS
Away, boy, from the troops, and save thyself,
For friends kill friends, and the disorder 's such
As war were hoodwinked.   16
IACHIMO   'Tis their fresh supplies.
LUCIUS
It is a day turned strangely ; or betimes   17
Let's reinforce or fly.   *Exeunt.*

V, ii   2 *off* away   3 *air on't* nature of it   4 *carl* peasant   8 *go before* excel
16 *hoodwinked* blindfolded   17 *or* either; *betimes* in time

V, iii   *Enter Posthumus and a Briton Lord.*

LORD
Cam'st thou from where they made the stand?

POSTHUMUS   I did;
Though you, it seems, come from the fliers.

LORD   I did.

POSTHUMUS
No blame be to you, sir, for all was lost,
But that the heavens fought. The King himself
Of his wings destitute, the army broken,
And but the backs of Britons seen, all flying

7   Through a strait lane; the enemy full-hearted,
8   Lolling the tongue with slaught'ring, having work
     More plentiful than tools to do't, struck down
10   Some mortally, some slightly touched, some falling
     Merely through fear, that the strait pass was dammed
12   With dead men hurt behind, and cowards living
     To die with length'ned shame.

LORD   Where was this lane?

POSTHUMUS
Close by the battle, ditched, and walled with turf;
Which gave advantage to an ancient soldier,
An honest one I warrant, who deserved

17   So long a breeding as his white beard came to,
     In doing this for's country. Athwart the lane
19   He with two striplings – lads more like to run
     The country base than to commit such slaughter;
21   With faces fit for masks, or rather fairer
22   Than those for preservation cased or shame –
     Made good the passage, cried to those that fled,
     'Our Britain's harts die flying, not our men.
25   To darkness fleet souls that fly backwards. Stand,

V, iii   **7** *strait* narrow; *full-hearted* with high morale   **8** *Lolling* letting
hang out   **10** *touched* wounded   **12** *behind* i.e. while running away   **17**
breeding life, support, cherishing   **19–20** *run ... base* play the game of
prisoner's base   **21** *fit for masks* delicate enough to justify protection
against the sun   **22** *for ... shame* covered for such protection or for
modesty   **25** *fleet* hurry

Or we are Romans and will give you that   26
Like beasts which you shun beastly, and may save   27
But to look back in frown. Stand, stand!' These three,
Three thousand confident, in act as many –
For three performers are the file when all   30
The rest do nothing – with this word 'Stand, stand,'
Accommodated by the place, more charming   32
With their own nobleness, which could have turned
A distaff to a lance, gilded pale looks,   34
Part shame, part spirit renewed; that some, turned   35
     coward
But by example – O, a sin in war,   36
Damned in the first beginners ! – gan to look   37
The way that they did and to grin like lions   38
Upon the pikes o' th' hunters. Then began
A stop i' th' chaser, a retire ; anon   40
A rout, confusion thick. Forthwith they fly
Chickens, the way which they stooped eagles ; slaves,   42
The strides they victors made ; and now our cowards,   43
Like fragments in hard voyages, became   44
The life o' th' need. Having found the backdoor open   45
Of the unguarded hearts, heavens, how they wound !
Some slain before, some dying, some their friends   47
O'erborne i' th' former wave, ten chased by one
Are now each one the slaughterman of twenty.

---

26 *we are Romans* we shall play the part of Romans   27 *beastly* i.e. like cowards   27–28 *save ... frown* prevent by looking back fiercely   30 *file* whole force   32 *Accommodated* given an advantage; *more charming* winning over others (to turn and fight)   34 *A distaff ... lance* a housewife into a soldier; *gilded* restored color to   35 *Part ... part* in some ... in others   36 *by example* by imitating others   37 *gan* began   37–38 *look The way* face in the direction   38 *they* i.e. Belarius and his sons; *grin* i.e. bare the teeth   40 *chaser* pursuer; *retire* retreat   42 *Chickens* like chickens; *way* route; *stooped eagles* swooped over like eagles; *slaves* like slaves (they fly back over)   43 *victors* as victors   44 *fragments* i.e. of food   45 *life ... need* support of life in time of need   45–46 *Having ... hearts* i.e. having found that the Romans were not invulnerable   47 *slain* i.e. having played dead; *dying* i.e. severely wounded; *their friends* friends of those already mentioned

50 Those that would die or ere resist are grown
51 The mortal bugs o' th' field.

LORD   This was strange chance:
A narrow lane, an old man, and two boys.

POSTHUMUS
Nay, do not wonder at it. You are made
Rather to wonder at the things you hear
55 Than to work any. Will you rhyme upon't
56 And vent it for a mock'ry? Here is one:
'Two boys, an old man twice a boy, a lane,
Preserved the Britons, was the Romans' bane.'

LORD
Nay, be not angry, sir.

59 POSTHUMUS   'Lack, to what end?
60 Who dares not stand his foe, I'll be his friend;
61 For if he'll do as he is made to do,
I know he'll quickly fly my friendship too.
63 You have put me into rhyme.

LORD   Farewell. You're angry. *Exit.*

POSTHUMUS
64 Still going? This is a lord! O noble misery,
To be i' th' field, and ask 'What news?' of me!
To-day how many would have given their honors
To have saved their carcasses, took heel to do't,
68 And yet died too! I, in mine own woe charmed,
Could not find Death where I did hear him groan
Nor feel him where he struck. Being an ugly monster,
71 'Tis strange he hides him in fresh cups, soft beds,
72 Sweet words, or hath moe ministers than we
That draw his knives i' th' war. Well, I will find him,
74 For being now a favorer to the Briton,

50 *or ere* rather than   51 *mortal bugs* deadly terrors (cf. 'bugbears')   55
work any perform such (things)   56 *vent it* air it, let it get around   59
'*Lack* alack, alas   60 *stand* withstand   61 *as ... do* as it is natural for him
to do   63 *put ... rhyme* made me versify   64 *going* running away; *noble
misery* wretchedness of a noble   68 *charmed* i.e. 'leading a charmed life'
71–72 *hides ... words* i.e. appears from unexpected places   72 *moe* more
74 *being ... favorer* death now favoring

No more a Briton. I have resumed again
The part I came in. Fight I will no more,   76
But yield me to the veriest hind that shall   77
Once touch my shoulder. Great the slaughter is   78
Here made by th' Roman; great the answer be   79
Britons must take. For me, my ransom's death.
On either side I come to spend my breath,   81
Which neither here I'll keep nor bear again,
But end it by some means for Imogen.
        Enter two [Briton] Captains and Soldiers.

I. CAPTAIN
Great Jupiter be praised, Lucius is taken.
'Tis thought the old man and his sons were angels.

2. CAPTAIN
There was a fourth man, in a silly habit,   86
That gave th' affront with them.   87

I. CAPTAIN   So 'tis reported,
But none of 'em can be found. Stand, who's there?

POSTHUMUS
A Roman,
Who had not now been drooping here if seconds   90
Had answered him.   91

2. CAPTAIN   Lay hands on him. A dog,
A leg of Rome shall not return to tell
What crows have pecked them here. He brags his service
As if he were of note. Bring him to th' King.
        Enter Cymbeline, Belarius, Guiderius, Arviragus,
        Pisanio, and Roman Captives. The Captains present
        Posthumus to Cymbeline, who delivers him over
        to a jailer.   [*Exeunt.*]

                            *

76 *part . . . in* i.e. his role as a Roman (as the way to find death, now helping
the British by taking their enemies)   77 *hind* peasant   78 *touch my shoulder*
i.e. as sign of arrest   79 *answer* retaliation   81 *spend my breath* yield my
life   86 *silly habit* simple garb   87 *affront* attack   90 *seconds* supporters
91 *answered him* acted as he did

V, iv   *Enter Posthumus and [two] Jailer[s].*

1. JAILER
You shall not now be stol'n; you have locks upon you.
So graze as you find pasture.

2. JAILER   Ay, or a stomach.

                                        [Exeunt Jailers.]

POSTHUMUS
Most welcome, bondage, for thou art a way,
I think, to liberty. Yet am I better
Than one that's sick o' th' gout, since he had rather
Groan so in perpetuity than be cured
By th' sure physician, Death, who is the key
T' unbar these locks. My conscience, thou art fettered
More than my shanks and wrists. You good gods, give me
10 The penitent instrument to pick that bolt,
11 Then free for ever. Is't enough I am sorry?
12 So children temporal fathers do appease;
    Gods are more full of mercy. Must I repent,
14 I cannot do it better than in gyves,
15 Desired more than constrained. To satisfy,
16 If of my freedom 'tis the main part, take
17 No stricter render of me than my all.
    I know you are more clement than vile men,
    Who of their broken debtors take a third,
    A sixth, a tenth, letting them thrive again
21 On their abatement. That's not my desire.
    For Imogen's dear life take mine; and though
    'Tis not so dear, yet 'tis a life; you coined it.
24 'Tween man and man they weigh not every stamp;
25 Though light, take pieces for the figure's sake;

V, iv A British stockade   10 *penitent ... bolt* penitence to unfetter his conscience   11 *free* i.e. in death   12 *So* i.e. by being sorry   14 *gyves* fetters   15 *constrained* forced upon me; *satisfy* atone   16 *If ... part* if it (atonement) is essential to my freedom (of conscience)   17 *stricter render* sterner repayment; *all* i.e. life   21 *abatement* reduced principal; *That* i.e. to thrive again   24 *stamp* coin   25 *figure's* i.e. of the royal image on the coin

You rather mine, being yours. And so, great pow'rs,   26
If you will take this audit, take this life   27
And cancel these cold bonds. O Imogen,   28
I'll speak to thee in silence.
    [Sleeps.]

    Solemn music. Enter, as in an apparition, Sicilius
    Leonatus, father to Posthumus, an old man attired
    like a warrior ; leading in his hand an ancient
    Matron, his wife and mother to Posthumus, with
    music before them. Then, after other music, follow
    the two young Leonati, brothers to Posthumus, with
    wounds as they died in the wars. They circle
    Posthumus round as he lies sleeping.

SICILIUS   No more, thou Thunder-master, show   30
       Thy spite on mortal flies.
    With Mars fall out, with Juno chide,
       That thy adulteries   33
          Rates and revenges.   34
    Hath my poor boy done aught but well,
       Whose face I never saw ?
    I died whilst in the womb he stayed
       Attending nature's law ;   38
    Whose father then, as men report
       Thou orphans' father art,
    Thou shouldst have been, and shielded him
       From this earth-vexing smart.   42

MOTHER   Lucina lent not me her aid,   43
       But took me in my throes,

---

26 *You ... yours* you more readily take my life (light coin though it is)
because you made it   **27** *take* accept   **28** *cold* heavy, depressing   **30**
Thunder-master Jupiter   **33** *That* who   **34** *Rates* scolds   **38** *Attending
nature's law* awaiting the completion of the natural process   **42** *earth-vexing
smart* suffering that afflicts earthly life   **43** *Lucina* goddess of childbirth

That from me was Posthumus ripped,
Came crying 'mongst his foes,
A thing of pity.

SICILIUS   Great Nature like his ancestry
49   Moulded the stuff so fair
That he deserved the praise o' th' world,
As great Sicilius' heir.

52 I. BROTHER   When once he was mature for man,
In Britain where was he
That could stand up his parallel,
55   Or fruitful object be
In eye of Imogen, that best
57   Could deem his dignity?

MOTHER   With marriage wherefore was he mocked,
To be exiled and thrown
From Leonati seat and cast
From her his dearest one,
Sweet Imogen?

63 SICILIUS   Why did you suffer Iachimo,
64   Slight thing of Italy,
65 To taint his nobler heart and brain
With needless jealousy,
67 And to become the geck and scorn
O' th' other's villainy?

69 2. BROTHER   For this from stiller seats we came,
Our parents and us twain,
71 That striking in our country's cause
Fell bravely and were slain,
Our fealty and Tenantius' right
With honor to maintain.

49 *stuff* substance (cf. I, i, 23)   52 *mature for man* grown up   55 *fruitful*
fulfilling potentialities   57 *deem his dignity* judge his worth   63 *suffer*
allow   64 *Slight* contemptible   65 *taint* infect   67 *geck* dupe   69 *stiller*
seats quieter dwelling places (Elysium)   71 *That* who

1. BROTHER	Like hardiment Posthumus hath	75
	To Cymbeline performed.	
	Then, Jupiter, thou king of gods,	
	Why hast thou thus adjourned	78
	The graces for his merits due,	
	Being all to dolors turned?	80

SICILIUS   Thy crystal window ope; look out.
             No longer exercise
             Upon a valiant race thy harsh
             And potent injuries.

MOTHER   Since, Jupiter, our son is good,
             Take off his miseries.   86

SICILIUS   Peep through thy marble mansion. Help,
             Or we poor ghosts will cry
             To th' shining synod of the rest   89
             Against thy deity.

BROTHERS   Help, Jupiter, or we appeal
             And from thy justice fly.

*Jupiter descends in thunder and lightning, sitting
upon an eagle. He throws a thunderbolt. The Ghosts
fall on their knees.*

JUPITER
No more, you petty spirits of region low,
    Offend our hearing. Hush! How dare you ghosts
Accuse the Thunderer, whose bolt, you know,
    Sky-planted, batters all rebelling coasts?   96
Poor shadows of Elysium, hence, and rest
    Upon your never-withering banks of flow'rs.
Be not with mortal accidents opprest.   99
    No care of yours it is; you know 'tis ours.

---

75 *hardiment* courageous deeds   78 *adjourned* put off   80 *dolors* sorrows
86 *off* away   89 *synod ... rest* assembly of the gods   96 *Sky-planted*
growing in the sky, based in the sky   99 *accidents* events

Whom best I love I cross ; to make my gift,
102   The more delayed, delighted. Be content.
Your low-laid son our godhead will uplift ;
104   His comforts thrive, his trials well are spent.
105 Our Jovial star reigned at his birth, and in
     Our temple was he married. Rise, and fade.
He shall be lord of Lady Imogen,
     And happier much by his affliction made.
This tablet lay upon his breast, wherein
110   Our pleasure his full fortune doth confine.
And so, away ; no farther with your din
     Express impatience, lest you stir up mine.
     Mount, eagle, to my palace crystalline.   *Ascends.*

SICILIUS
He came in thunder ; his celestial breath
Was sulphurous to smell ; the holy eagle
116 Stooped, as to foot us. His ascension is
117 More sweet than our blest fields ; his royal bird
118 Prunes the immortal wing and cloys his beak,
As when his god is pleased.
ALL   Thanks, Jupiter.
SICILIUS
120 The marble pavement closes ; he is entered
His radiant roof. Away, and, to be blest,
Let us with care perform his great behest.
                        [The Ghosts] vanish.
POSTHUMUS *[waking]*
Sleep, thou hast been a grandsire and begot
A father to me, and thou hast created
125 A mother and two brothers ; but, O scorn,
Gone ! They went hence so soon as they were born.

102 *delighted* (the more) delighted in   104 *spent* ended   105 *Jovial star*
planet Jupiter, supposed to bring good fortune   110 *confine* set down con-
cisely   116 *Stooped . . . foot* swooped as if to seize (with claws)   117 *More*
sweet i.e. in contrast with the sulphurous descent   118 *Prunes* trims; *cloys*
claws   120 *marble pavement* i.e. heaven   125 *O scorn* what a bitter joke

And so I am awake. Poor wretches that depend
On greatness' favor, dream as I have done;
Wake, and find nothing. But, alas, I swerve.   129
Many dream not to find, neither deserve,
And yet are steeped in favors. So am I,
That have this golden chance and know not why.
What fairies haunt this ground? A book? O rare one,   133
Be not, as is our fangled world, a garment   134
Nobler than that it covers. Let thy effects   135
So follow to be most unlike our courtiers,   136
As good as promise.
        Reads.
'When as a lion's whelp shall, to himself unknown,   138
without seeking find, and be embraced by a piece of   139
tender air; and when from a stately cedar shall be lopped
branches which, being dead many years, shall after
revive, be jointed to the old stock, and freshly grow;
then shall Posthumus end his miseries, Britain be for-
tunate and flourish in peace and plenty.'
'Tis still a dream, or else such stuff as madmen
Tongue, and brain not; either both, or nothing,   146
Or senseless speaking, or a speaking such   147
As sense cannot untie. Be what it is,
The action of my life is like it, which   149
I'll keep, if but for sympathy.   150
        Enter Jailer.
JAILER Come, sir, are you ready for death?
POSTHUMUS Over-roasted rather; ready long ago.
JAILER Hanging is the word, sir. If you be ready for that,   153
    you are well cooked.

---

129 *swerve* err (cf. 'I'm off the track')   133 *book* i.e. the *tablet* of l. 109
134 *fangled* dressy, fancy   135 *effects* fulfillment   136 *to* as to   138 *When*
as when   139 *piece* creature, morsel   146 *Tongue* say; *brain* understand
147 *senseless* irrational   147–48 *such . . . untie* too cryptic for rational
analysis   149 *like it* i.e. in being difficult to understand   150 *sympathy*
resemblance   153 *Hanging* (pun on death by hanging and hanging up of
meat)

POSTHUMUS So, if I prove a good repast to the specta-
156 tors, the dish pays the shot.

JAILER A heavy reckoning for you, sir. But the comfort is,
you shall be called to no more payments, fear no more
159 tavern bills, which are often the sadness of parting, as
the procuring of mirth. You come in faint for want of
meat, depart reeling with too much drink; sorry that
162 you have paid too much, and sorry that you are paid too
much; purse and brain both empty; the brain the heavi-
164 er for being too light, the purse too light, being drawn of
heaviness. O, of this contradiction you shall now be quit.
166 O, the charity of a penny cord! It sums up thousands in
167 a trice. You have no true debitor and creditor but it; of
168 what's past, is, and to come, the discharge. Your neck, sir,
169 is pen, book, and counters; so the acquittance follows.
170 POSTHUMUS I am merrier to die than thou art to live.

JAILER Indeed, sir, he that sleeps feels not the toothache;
172 but a man that were to sleep your sleep, and a hangman
to help him to bed, I think he would change places with
174 his officer; for look you, sir, you know not which way
you shall go.

POSTHUMUS Yes indeed do I, fellow.

JAILER Your death has eyes in's head then. I have not
178 seen him so pictured. You must either be directed by
179 some that take upon them to know, or to take upon
180 yourself that which I am sure you do not know, or jump
181 the after-inquiry on your own peril. And how you shall
182 speed in your journey's end, I think you'll never return
to tell one.

---

156 *dish* food; *shot* reckoning   159 *often* as often   162 *are paid* are paid
off, punished (by too much liquor)   164 *drawn* emptied   166 *cord* i.e. for
hanging   167 *debitor and creditor* accountant   168 *discharge* payment
169 *counters* round pieces of metal used for reckoning; *acquittance* receipt
170 *to die ... to live* in dying ... in living   172 *a man that were* as for a man
scheduled   174 *officer* i.e. the hangman   178 *so pictured* i.e. in the
conventional skull representing death   179 *some* clergy (?)   179–80 *take
upon yourself* decide for yourself (on your salvation)   180 *jump* gamble on
181 *after-inquiry* final judgment   182 *speed in* make out at

POSTHUMUS I tell thee, fellow, there are none want eyes
to direct them the way I am going but such as wink and 185
will not use them.

JAILER What an infinite mock is this, that a man should 187
have the best use of eyes to see the way of blindness! I
am sure hanging's the way of winking.

    Enter a Messenger.

MESSENGER Knock off his manacles; bring your prisoner
to the King.

POSTHUMUS Thou bring'st good news; I am called to be
made free.   193

JAILER I'll be hanged then.

POSTHUMUS Thou shalt be then freer than a jailer. No
bolts for the dead. *Exeunt [Posthumus and Messenger].*

JAILER Unless a man would marry a gallows and beget
young gibbets, I never saw one so prone. Yet, on my 198
conscience, there are verier knaves desire to live, for all
he be a Roman; and there be some of them too that die
against their wills. So should I, if I were one. I would we
were all of one mind, and one mind good. O, there were
desolation of jailers and gallowses! I speak against my
present profit, but my wish hath a preferment in't. 204
                                       [Exit.]

                  *

    Enter Cymbeline, Belarius, Guiderius, Arviragus,   V, v
    Pisanio, and Lords.

CYMBELINE
    Stand by my side, you whom the gods have made
    Preservers of my throne. Woe is my heart
    That the poor soldier that so richly fought,
    Whose rags shamed gilded arms, whose naked breast
    Stepped before targes of proof, cannot be found.   5

---

185 *wink* close   187 *mock* joke   193 *made free* i.e. by death   198 *prone*
inclined (to die)   204 *hath . . . in't* includes a better position for myself
V, v The camp of King Cymbeline   5 *targes of proof* shields of proved
strength

He shall be happy that can find him, if
Our grace can make him so.

BELARIUS   I never saw
Such noble fury in so poor a thing,
9 Such precious deeds in one that promised naught
But beggary and poor looks.

CYMBELINE   No tidings of him?

PISANIO
He hath been searched among the dead and living,
But no trace of him.

CYMBELINE   To my grief, I am
The heir of his reward, *[to Belarius, Guiderius, and Ar-*
viragus] which I will add
14 To you, the liver, heart, and brain of Britain,
15 By whom I grant she lives. 'Tis now the time
To ask of whence you are. Report it.

BELARIUS   Sir,
In Cambria are we born, and gentlemen.
Further to boast were neither true nor modest,
Unless I add we are honest.

CYMBELINE   Bow your knees.
20 Arise my knights o' th' battle; I create you
21 Companions to our person and will fit you
22 With dignities becoming your estates.
Enter Cornelius and Ladies.
23 There's business in these faces. Why so sadly
Greet you our victory? You look like Romans
And not o' th' court of Britain.

CORNELIUS   Hail, great King!
To sour your happiness I must report
The Queen is dead.

27 CYMBELINE   Who worse than a physician

---

9 *promised* offered, presented   14 *the liver … brain* who are the vital parts
15 *she* Britain   20 *knights … battle* knights created on the battlefield (cf.
'battlefield commission')   21 *fit* equip   22 *estates* status as knights   23
There's … faces i.e. their looks show that these persons have something
important to tell   27 *Who* (for 'whom')

Would this report become? But I consider
By med'cine life may be prolonged, yet death
Will seize the doctor too. How ended she?

CORNELIUS
With horror, madly dying, like her life,
Which, being cruel to the world, concluded
Most cruel to herself. What she confessed
I will report, so please you. These her women
Can trip me if I err, who with wet cheeks   35
Were present when she finished.

CYMBELINE   Prithee say.

CORNELIUS
First, she confessed she never loved you, only
Affected greatness got by you, not you;   38
Married your royalty, was wife to your place,
Abhorred your person.   40

CYMBELINE   She alone knew this,
And but she spoke it dying, I would not   41
Believe her lips in opening it. Proceed.   42

CORNELIUS
Your daughter, whom she bore in hand to love   43
With such integrity, she did confess
Was as a scorpion to her sight, whose life,
But that her flight prevented it, she had
Ta'en off by poison.   47

CYMBELINE   O most delicate fiend!
Who is't can read a woman? Is there more?

CORNELIUS
More, sir, and worse. She did confess she had
For you a mortal mineral, which, being took,   50
Should by the minute feed on life and, ling'ring,   51
By inches waste you. In which time she purposed,   52

---

35 *trip* stop, catch   38 *Affected* desired, loved   40 *your* you as a   41 *but*
but for the fact that   42 *opening* disclosing   43 *bore in hand* pretended
47 *Ta'en off* destroyed; *delicate* subtle   50 *mortal mineral* deadly poison
51 *by the minute* minute by minute   52 *waste* consume, destroy.

53 By watching, weeping, tendance, kissing, to
54 O'ercome you with her show and, in time,
55 When she had fitted you with her craft, to work
56 Her son into th' adoption of the crown;
But failing of her end by his strange absence,
Grew shameless desperate, opened, in despite
59 Of heaven and men, her purposes, repented
The evils she hatched were not effected, so
Despairing died.

CYMBELINE   Heard you all this, her women?

LADY
We did, so please your Highness.

CYMBELINE   Mine eyes
Were not in fault, for she was beautiful;
Mine ears, that heard her flattery; nor my heart,
65 That thought her like her seeming. It had been vicious
To have mistrusted her. Yet, O my daughter,
67 That it was folly in me thou mayst say,
68 And prove it in thy feeling. Heaven mend all!

*Enter Lucius, Iachimo, [the Soothsayer,] and other
Roman Prisoners, [Posthumus] Leonatus behind,
and Imogen.*

Thou com'st not, Caius, now for tribute. That
70 The Britons have razed out, though with the loss
Of many a bold one; whose kinsmen have made suit
72 That their good souls may be appeased with slaughter
Of you their captives, which ourself have granted.
74 So think of your estate.

LUCIUS
Consider, sir, the chance of war. The day
76 Was yours by accident; had it gone with us,
We should not, when the blood was cool, have threatened

53 *tendance* attentiveness   54 *show* pretense (of devotion)   55 *fitted*
shaped to her purpose   56 *adoption of* adoption by you as heir to   59
repented was bitterly sorry because   65 *seeming* appearance; *had been
vicious* would have been a fault   67 *it* i.e. trusting her   68 *prove*
experience; *feeling* suffering   70 *razed out* erased   72 *their* i.e. of those
lost in battle   74 *estate* spiritual state   76 *had . . . us* had we won

Our prisoners with the sword. But since the gods
Will have it thus, that nothing but our lives
May be called ransom, let it come. Sufficeth
A Roman with a Roman's heart can suffer.
Augustus lives to think on't – and so much
For my peculiar care. This one thing only   83
I will entreat : my boy, a Briton born,
Let him be ransomed. Never master had
A page so kind, so duteous, diligent,
So tender over his occasions, true,   87
So feat, so nurse-like. Let his virtue join   88
With my request, which I'll make bold your Highness
Cannot deny. He hath done no Briton harm,
Though he have served a Roman. Save him, sir,
And spare no blood beside.   92
CYMBELINE   I have surely seen him ;
His favor is familiar to me. Boy,   93
Thou hast looked thyself into my grace   94
And art mine own. I know not why, wherefore,   95
To say 'Live, boy.' Ne'er thank thy master. Live,
And ask of Cymbeline what boon thou wilt,
Fitting my bounty and thy state ; I'll give it,   98
Yea, though thou do demand a prisoner,
The noblest ta'en.
IMOGEN   I humbly thank your Highness.
LUCIUS
I do not bid thee beg my life, good lad,
And yet I know thou wilt.
IMOGEN   No, no, alack,
There's other work in hand. I see a thing   103
Bitter to me as death ; your life, good master,
Must shuffle for itself.   105

83 *my peculiar care* care for myself   87 *tender ... occasions* sensitive to his
(master's) wants   88 *feat* skillful   92 *no blood beside* the blood of no one
else   93 *favor* face   94 *looked ... grace* by your looks secured my mercy
95 *I ... wherefore* (cf. 'I don't know why I'm doing it'; hence, 'You need
not thank Lucius')   98 *Fitting* appropriate to   103 *thing* (cf. ll. 135-36)
105 *shuffle* make out as best it can

LUCIUS   The boy disdains me;
106   He leaves me, scorns me. Briefly die their joys
107   That place them on the truth of girls and boys.
108   Why stands he so perplexed?
CYMBELINE   What wouldst thou, boy?
I love thee more and more. Think more and more
What's best to ask. Know'st him thou look'st on? Speak.
Wilt have him live? Is he thy kin? Thy friend?
IMOGEN
He is a Roman, no more kin to me
Than I to your Highness; who, being born your vassal,
114   Am something nearer.
CYMBELINE   Wherefore ey'st him so?
IMOGEN
I'll tell you, sir, in private, if you please
To give me hearing.
CYMBELINE   Ay, with all my heart,
And lend my best attention. What's thy name?
IMOGEN
Fidele, sir.
CYMBELINE   Thou'rt my good youth, my page;
I'll be thy master. Walk with me; speak freely.
    [Cymbeline and Imogen talk apart.]
BELARIUS
Is not this boy revived from death?
ARVIRAGUS   One sand another
121   Not more resembles that sweet rosy lad
Who died, and was Fidele. What think you?
GUIDERIUS
The same dead thing alive.
BELARIUS
Peace, peace, see further. He eyes us not; forbear.

106 *Briefly* soon   106–07 *their joys That* the joys of those who   107 *place
... truth* make them depend on the fidelity   108 *perplexed* troubled   114
something nearer somewhat closer (to you than he is to me)   121 *Not ...
lad* (unusually elliptical; some words may be lost)

Creatures may be alike. Were't he, I am sure
He would have spoke to us.

GUIDERIUS   But we see him dead.   126

BELARIUS
Be silent; let's see further.

PISANIO *[aside]*   It is my mistress.
Since she is living, let the time run on
To good or bad.
[Cymbeline and Imogen advance.]

CYMBELINE   Come, stand thou by our side;
Make thy demand aloud. *[to Iachimo]* Sir, step you forth,
Give answer to this boy, and do it freely;
Or, by our greatness and the grace of it,   132
Which is our honor, bitter torture shall
Winnow the truth from falsehood. – On, speak to him.

IMOGEN
My boon is that this gentleman may render   135
Of whom he had this ring.

POSTHUMUS *[aside]*   What's that to him?

CYMBELINE
That diamond upon your finger, say
How came it yours.

IACHIMO
Thou'lt torture me to leave unspoken that   139
Which to be spoke would torture thee.

CYMBELINE   How? Me?

IACHIMO
I am glad to be constrained to utter that
Which torments me to conceal. By villainy
I got this ring. 'Twas Leonatus' jewel,
Whom thou didst banish, and – which more may grieve
    thee,
As it doth me – a nobler sir ne'er lived
'Twixt sky and ground. Wilt thou hear more, my lord?

126 *But ... dead* unless we see him dead (?), but what we see is a ghost
(?)   132–33 *grace ... honor* our honor, which embellishes (our greatness)
135 *render* tell   139 *to leave* for leaving

CYMBELINE
All that belongs to this.

IACHIMO   That paragon, thy daughter,
For whom my heart drops blood and my false spirits
Quail to remember – Give me leave ; I faint.

CYMBELINE
My daughter ? What of her ? Renew thy strength.
151 I had rather thou shouldst live while nature will
Than die ere I hear more. Strive, man, and speak.

IACHIMO
Upon a time – unhappy was the clock
That struck the hour ! – it was in Rome – accursed
The mansion where ! – 'twas at a feast – O, would
Our viands had been poisoned, or at least
157 Those which I heaved to head ! – the good Posthumus –
What should I say ? He was too good to be
Where ill men were, and was the best of all
Amongst the rar'st of good ones – sitting sadly,
Hearing us praise our loves of Italy
162 For beauty that made barren the swelled boast
163 Of him that best could speak ; for feature, laming
164 The shrine of Venus or straight-pight Minerva,
165 Postures beyond brief nature ; for condition,
166 A shop of all the qualities that man
167 Loves woman for ; besides that hook of wiving,
Fairness which strikes the eye –

CYMBELINE   I stand on fire.
169 Come to the matter.

IACHIMO   All too soon I shall,
Unless thou wouldst grieve quickly. This Posthumus,
Most like a noble lord in love and one

151 *while nature will* i.e. your natural life   157 *heaved to head* raised to
mouth   162 *made … boast* rendered even an exaggerated boast powerless
(to express)   163 *feature* figure; *laming* making a cripple of   164 *shrine*
image; *straight-pight* erect   165 *Postures* forms; *beyond brief nature* of
immortal beings (?), more enduring (as art) than natural beings (?); *condition* character   166 *shop* store   167 *hook* i.e. fishhook; *of wiving* for
marriage   169 *matter* point

That had a royal lover, took his hint,   172
And not dispraising whom we praised – therein
He was as calm as virtue – he began
His mistress' picture; which by his tongue being made,
And then a mind put in't, either our brags   176
Were cracked of kitchen trulls, or his description   177
Proved us unspeaking sots.   178
CYMBELINE   Nay, nay, to th' purpose.
IACHIMO
Your daughter's chastity – there it begins.
He spake of her as Dian had hot dreams   180
And she alone were cold; whereat I, wretch,   181
Made scruple of his praise and wagered with him   182
Pieces of gold 'gainst this which then he wore
Upon his honored finger, to attain
In suit the place of's bed and win this ring   185
By hers and mine adultery. He, true knight,
No lesser of her honor confident
Than I did truly find her, stakes this ring;
And would so, had it been a carbuncle   189
Of Phoebus' wheel, and might so safely, had it   190
Been all the worth of's car. Away to Britain
Post I in this design. Well may you, sir,   192
Remember me at court, where I was taught
Of your chaste daughter the wide difference   194
'Twixt amorous and villainous. Being thus quenched   195
Of hope, not longing, mine Italian brain
Gan in your duller Britain operate   197
Most vilely; for my vantage, excellent.   198

---

172 *lover* woman in love with him; *hint* opportunity   **176** *mind put in't* i.e.
she had brains as well as beauty   **177** *cracked of* boasted about; *trulls*
wenches   **178** *unspeaking sots* inarticulate fools; *to th' purpose* (keep) to the
point   **180** *as* as if; *hot* lecherous   **181** *cold* chaste   **182** *Made scruple of*
stated disbelief in   **185** *In suit* by wooing   **189** *would so* would have done so
190 *Phoebus' wheel* i.e. wheel on the sun's chariot; *might so* might have done
so   **192** *Post* hurry   **194** *Of* by   **195** *amorous* faithful love   **195–96**
quenched Of cooled off in   **197** *duller Britain* (northern countries
supposedly produced slower minds)   **198** *vantage* profit

199 And, to be brief, my practice so prevailed
200 That I returned with simular proof enough
To make the noble Leonatus mad
202 By wounding his belief in her renown
203 With tokens thus and thus; averring notes
Of chamber hanging, pictures, this her bracelet –
O cunning, how I got it! – nay, some marks
Of secret on her person, that he could not
207 But think her bond of chastity quite cracked,
208 I having ta'en the forfeit. Whereupon –
Methinks I see him now –
POSTHUMUS *[advancing]* Ay, so thou dost,
Italian fiend! Ay me, most credulous fool,
211 Egregious murderer, thief, anything
That's due to all the villains past, in being,
To come! O, give me cord or knife or poison,
214 Some upright justicer! Thou, King, send out
For torturers ingenious. It is I
216 That all th' abhorrèd things o' th' earth amend
By being worse than they. I am Posthumus,
That killed thy daughter – villain-like, I lie –
That caused a lesser villain than myself,
A sacrilegious thief, to do't. The temple
221 Of virtue was she; yea, and she herself.
Spit, and throw stones, cast mire upon me, set
The dogs o' th' street to bay me; every villain
Be called Posthumus Leonatus, and
225 Be villainy less than 'twas! O Imogen!
My queen, my life, my wife! O Imogen,
Imogen, Imogen!
IMOGEN   Peace, my lord. Hear, hear –

---

199 *practice* scheming   200 *simular* simulated   202 *renown* good name
203 *averring notes* affirming the marks   207 *cracked* broken   208 *ta'en the
forfeit* gained what was forfeited (by breach of bond)   211 *anything* i.e.
any name   214 *justicer* judge   216 *amend* make (seem) better   221 *she
herself* virtue herself   225 *Be . . . 'twas* i.e. I have made other villainies
seem smaller

POSTHUMUS
  Shall's have a play of this? Thou scornful page,   228
  There lie thy part.   229
      [Thrusts her away; she falls.]
PISANIO   O gentlemen, help!
  Mine and your mistress! O my lord Posthumus,
  You ne'er killed Imogen till now. Help, help!
  Mine honored lady!
CYMBELINE   Does the world go round?
POSTHUMUS
  How come these staggers on me?   233
PISANIO   Wake, my mistress!
CYMBELINE
  If this be so, the gods do mean to strike me
  To death with mortal joy.   235
PISANIO   How fares my mistress?
IMOGEN
  O, get thee from my sight;
  Thou gav'st me poison. Dangerous fellow, hence;
  Breathe not where princes are.
CYMBELINE   The tune of Imogen!   238
PISANIO
  Lady,
  The gods throw stones of sulphur on me if   240
  That box I gave you was not thought by me
  A precious thing; I had it from the Queen.   242
CYMBELINE
  New matter still.   243
IMOGEN   It poisoned me.
CORNELIUS   O gods!
  I left out one thing which the Queen confessed,
  Which must approve thee honest. 'If Pisanio   245

228 *Shall's* shall we 229 *There . . . part* lying there is your role 233 *staggers* dizziness, agitation 235 *mortal* fatal 238 *tune* voice 240 *stones of sulphur* thunderbolts 242 *precious* beneficial 243 *matter* developments 245 *approve* prove; *honest* truthful

246   Have,' said she, 'given his mistress that confection
          Which I gave him for cordial, she is served
          As I would serve a rat.'

CYMBELINE   What's this, Cornelius?

CORNELIUS
          The Queen, sir, very oft importuned me
250   To temper poisons for her, still pretending
          The satisfaction of her knowledge only
          In killing creatures vile, as cats and dogs
253   Of no esteem. I, dreading that her purpose
254   Was of more danger, did compound for her
255   A certain stuff which, being ta'en, would cease
          The present pow'r of life, but in short time
257   All offices of nature should again
          Do their due functions. Have you ta'en of it?

IMOGEN
259   Most like I did, for I was dead.

BELARIUS   My boys,
          There was our error.

GUIDERIUS   This is sure Fidele.

IMOGEN
          Why did you throw your wedded lady from you?
262   Think that you are upon a rock, and now
263   Throw me again.
            [Embraces him.]

POSTHUMUS   Hang there like fruit, my soul,
          Till the tree die!

CYMBELINE   How now, my flesh, my child?
265   What, mak'st thou me a dullard in this act?
          Wilt thou not speak to me?

---

246 *confection* mixture   250 *temper* mix; *pretending* alleging as her purpose   253 *esteem* value   254 *of more danger* more harmful   255 *cease* cut off   257 *offices of nature* bodily parts   259 *like* probably; *dead* as if dead   262 *rock* i.e. firm ground (?) (sometimes emended to 'lock' and explained as a metaphor from wrestling)   263 *Throw me again* i.e. if you can (we are now inseparable)   265 *dullard* i.e. by ignoring me (and giving me no lines to speak); *act* perhaps, play (cf. ll. 228–29)

IMOGEN *[kneeling]*   Your blessing, sir.
BELARIUS *[to Guiderius and Arviragus]*
  Though you did love this youth, I blame ye not;
  You had a motive for't.   268
CYMBELINE   My tears that fall
  Prove holy water on thee. Imogen,
  Thy mother's dead.
IMOGEN   I am sorry for't, my lord.
CYMBELINE
  O, she was naught, and long of her it was   271
  That we meet here so strangely; but her son
  Is gone, we know not how nor where.
PISANIO   My lord,
  Now fear is from me, I'll speak troth. Lord Cloten,   274
  Upon my lady's missing, came to me
  With his sword drawn, foamed at the mouth, and swore,
  If I discovered not which way she was gone,   277
  It was my instant death. By accident
  I had a feignèd letter of my master's   279
  Then in my pocket, which directed him
  To seek her on the mountains near to Milford;
  Where, in a frenzy, in my master's garments,
  Which he enforced from me, away he posts
  With unchaste purpose and with oath to violate
  My lady's honor. What became of him
  I further know not.
GUIDERIUS   Let me end the story:
  I slew him there.
CYMBELINE   Marry, the gods forfend!   287
  I would not thy good deeds should from my lips   288
  Pluck a hard sentence. Prithee, valiant youth,
  Deny't again.   290

---

268 *motive* cause   **271** *naught* evil; *long of* because of   **274** *troth* truth
277 *discovered* revealed   **279** *letter* (cf. III, v, 99–100)   **287** *forfend* forbid
288 *thy good deeds* (that after) thy good deeds (against the Romans, thou)
290 *again* against (what you have just said)

GUIDERIUS   I have spoke it, and I did it.

CYMBELINE
He was a prince.

GUIDERIUS
A most incivil one. The wrongs he did me
Were nothing princelike, for he did provoke me
With language that would make me spurn the sea
If it could so roar to me. I cut off's head,
And am right glad he is not standing here
297   To tell this tale of mine.

CYMBELINE   I am sorrow for thee.
By thine own tongue thou art condemned and must
Endure our law. Thou'rt dead.

IMOGEN   That headless man
I thought had been my lord.

CYMBELINE   Bind the offender
And take him from our presence.

BELARIUS   Stay, sir King.
This man is better than the man he slew,
As well descended as thyself, and hath
More of thee merited than a band of Clotens
305   Had ever scar for. *[to the Guard]* Let his arms alone;
They were not born for bondage.

CYMBELINE   Why, old soldier,
Wilt thou undo the worth thou art unpaid for
By tasting of our wrath? How of descent
As good as we?

ARVIRAGUS   In that he spake too far.

CYMBELINE
310   And thou shalt die for't.

BELARIUS   We will die all three
311   But I will prove that two on's are as good
As I have given out him. My sons, I must

---

297 *tell . . . mine* i.e. report that he cut off my head; *sorrow* (a possible idiom; some editors emend to 'sorry')   305 *Had . . . for* earned by battle wounds   310 *thou* i.e. Belarius   311 *But* unless

For mine own part unfold a dangerous speech, 313
Though haply well for you.
ARVIRAGUS   Your danger's ours.
GUIDERIUS
And our good his.
BELARIUS   Have at it then. By leave, 315
Thou hadst, great King, a subject who
Was called Belarius.
CYMBELINE   What of him? He is
A banished traitor.
BELARIUS   He it is that hath
Assumed this age; indeed a banished man, 319
I know not how a traitor.
CYMBELINE   Take him hence.
The whole world shall not save him.
BELARIUS   Not too hot. 321
First pay me for the nursing of thy sons,
And let it be confiscate all, so soon 323
As I have received it.
CYMBELINE   Nursing of my sons?
BELARIUS
I am too blunt and saucy; here's my knee. 325
Ere I arise I will prefer my sons; 326
Then spare not the old father. Mighty sir,
These two young gentlemen that call me father
And think they are my sons are none of mine;
They are the issue of your loins, my liege,
And blood of your begetting.
CYMBELINE   How? My issue?
BELARIUS
So sure as you your father's. I, old Morgan,
Am that Belarius whom you sometime banished. 333

313 *For ... speech* make an explanatory statement dangerous to myself
315 *Have at it* let's go ahead; *By leave* by your permission   319 *Assumed
this age* taken on this look of age   321 *hot* hasty   323 *it* the payment   325
saucy direct, 'fresh'   326 *prefer* advance   333 *sometime* once

334 Your pleasure was my mere offense, my punishment
Itself, and all my treason; that I suffered
Was all the harm I did. These gentle princes–
For such and so they are–these twenty years
338 Have I trained up; those arts they have as I
Could put into them. My breeding was, sir, as
Your Highness knows. Their nurse, Euriphile,
Whom for the theft I wedded, stole these children
342 Upon my banishment. I moved her to't,
Having received the punishment before
344 For that which I did then. Beaten for loyalty
Excited me to treason. Their dear loss,
346 The more of you 'twas felt, the more it shaped
Unto my end of stealing them. But, gracious sir,
Here are your sons again, and I must lose
Two of the sweet'st companions in the world.
The benediction of these covering heavens
Fall on their heads like dew, for they are worthy
To inlay heaven with stars.
CYMBELINE   Thou weep'st and speak'st.
353 The service that you three have done is more
354 Unlike than this thou tell'st. I lost my children;
If these be they, I know not how to wish
A pair of worthier sons.
BELARIUS   Be pleased awhile.
This gentleman whom I call Polydore,
Most worthy prince, as yours, is true Guiderius;
This gentleman, my Cadwal, Arviragus,
360 Your younger princely son. He, sir, was lapped
361 In a most curious mantle, wrought by th' hand
362 Of his queen mother, which for more probation
I can with ease produce.

334-35 *Your . . . treason* my whole offense, etc., existed only because it
pleased you (to declare them) 338 *arts* accomplishments 342 *moved*
incited 344 *Beaten* being beaten 346 *of* by 346-47 *shaped . . . of*
served my end in 353 *service* i.e. in battle 354 *Unlike* improbable 360
lapped wrapped 361 *curious* artfully wrought 362 *probation* proof

CYMBELINE   Guiderius had
Upon his neck a mole, a sanguine star;   364
It was a mark of wonder.
BELARIUS   This is he,
Who hath upon him still that natural stamp.
It was wise Nature's end in the donation   367
To be his evidence now.   368
CYMBELINE   O, what am I?
A mother to the birth of three? Ne'er mother
Rejoiced deliverance more. Blest pray you be,
That, after this strange starting from your orbs,   371
You may reign in them now! O Imogen,
Thou hast lost by this a kingdom.
IMOGEN   No, my lord,
I have got two worlds by't. O my gentle brothers,
Have we thus met? O, never say hereafter
But I am truest speaker. You called me brother
When I was but your sister, I you brothers
When we were so indeed.
CYMBELINE   Did you e'er meet?
ARVIRAGUS
Ay, my good lord.
GUIDERIUS   And at first meeting loved,
Continued so until we thought he died.
CORNELIUS
By the Queen's dram she swallowed.
CYMBELINE   O rare instinct!
When shall I hear all through? This fierce abridgment   382
Hath to it circumstantial branches, which   383
Distinction should be rich in. Where, how lived you?
And when came you to serve our Roman captive?
How parted with your brothers? How first met them?

364 *sanguine* blood-red   367 *end* purpose; *donation* endowing (him with
the mark)   368 *his evidence* evidence of his identity   371 *orbs* orbits   382
fierce abridgment extraordinary pastime   383 *branches* ramifications, details
383–84 *which … in* which, as they are distinguished, should be plentiful

Why fled you from the court? And whither? These,
388 And your three motives to the battle, with
I know not how much more, should be demanded,
390 And all the other by-dependences
391 From chance to chance; but nor the time nor place
392 Will serve our long interrogatories. See,
Posthumus anchors upon Imogen,
And she like harmless lightning throws her eye
On him, her brothers, me, her master, hitting
396 Each object with a joy; the counterchange
397 Is severally in all. Let's quit this ground
398 And smoke the temple with our sacrifices.
      [To Belarius]
399 Thou art my brother; so we'll hold thee ever.

IMOGEN
400 You are my father too, and did relieve me
401 To see this gracious season.

CYMBELINE   All o'erjoyed
Save these in bonds; let them be joyful too,
403 For they shall taste our comfort.

IMOGEN   My good master,
I will yet do you service.

LUCIUS   Happy be you!

CYMBELINE
405 The forlorn soldier, that so nobly fought,
He would have well becomed this place and graced
The thankings of a king.

POSTHUMUS   I am, sir,
The soldier that did company these three
409 In poor beseeming; 'twas a fitment for

---

388 *your three motives* what impelled you three   390 *by-dependences* related matters   391 *chance* happening   392 *Will serve* are suited to   396 *counterchange* exchange   397 *Is . . . all* i.e. all engage in it, each according to his relationship to the others   398 *smoke* fill with incense   399 *hold* regard   400 *You* i.e. Belarius; *relieve* aid   401 *gracious season* joyful occasion   403 *taste our comfort* share in our well-being   405 *forlorn* missing   **409** *beseeming* appearance (i.e. garb); *fitment for* garb fitted for

The purpose I then followed. That I was he, 410
Speak, Iachimo. I had you down and might
Have made you finish. 412

IACHIMO *[kneeling]* I am down again,
But now my heavy conscience sinks my knee, 413
As then your force did. Take that life, beseech you,
Which I so often owe; but your ring first, 415
And here the bracelet of the truest princess
That ever swore her faith.

POSTHUMUS Kneel not to me.
The pow'r that I have on you is to spare you;
The malice towards you to forgive you. Live,
And deal with others better.

CYMBELINE Nobly doomed! 420
We'll learn our freeness of a son-in-law: 421
Pardon's the word to all.

ARVIRAGUS You holp us, sir,
As you did mean indeed to be our brother.
Joyed are we that you are. 424

POSTHUMUS
Your servant, princes. Good my lord of Rome,
Call forth your soothsayer. As I slept, methought
Great Jupiter, upon his eagle backed, 427
Appeared to me, with other spritely shows 428
Of mine own kindred. When I waked, I found
This label on my bosom, whose containing 430
Is so from sense in hardness that I can 431
Make no collection of it. Let him show 432
His skill in the construction. 433

LUCIUS Philarmonus!

---

410 *followed* was carrying out **412** *finish* die **413** *sinks* makes bend **415** *often* many times (because of the extent of my misdeeds) **420** *doomed* judged **421** *freeness* generosity **424** *you are* i.e. our brother **427** *upon . . . backed* on the back of his eagle **428** *spritely shows* ghostly visions **430** *label* piece of paper; *containing* contents **431** *from . . . hardness* hard to understand **432** *collection* elucidation **433** *construction* construing, interpreting (of it)

SOOTHSAYER
  Here, my good lord.
  LUCIUS   Read, and declare the meaning.
  SOOTHSAYER *[reads]* 'When as a lion's whelp shall, to
    himself unknown, without seeking find, and be em-
    braced by a piece of tender air; and when from a stately
    cedar shall be lopped branches which, being dead many
    years, shall after revive, be jointed to the old stock, and
    freshly grow; then shall Posthumus end his miseries,
    Britain be fortunate and flourish in peace and plenty.'
          [To Leonatus]
    Thou, Leonatus, art the lion's whelp;
    The fit and apt construction of thy name,
444 Being *Leo-natus*, doth import so much.
          [To Cymbeline]
    The piece of tender air, thy virtuous daughter,
446 Which we call 'mollis aer,' and 'mollis aer'
    We term it 'mulier'; which 'mulier' I divine
    Is this most constant wife, who even now
449 Answering the letter of the oracle,
          [To Posthumus]
450 Unknown to you, unsought, were clipped about
    With this most tender air.
451 CYMBELINE   This hath some seeming.
  SOOTHSAYER
    The lofty cedar, royal Cymbeline,
453 Personates thee, and thy lopped branches point
    Thy two sons forth; who, by Belarius stol'n,
    For many years thought dead, are now revived,
456 To the majestic cedar joined, whose issue
    Promises Britain peace and plenty.

---

444 *Leo-natus* lion-born; *import* mean, imply   446 *mollis aer* tender air (a
supposed origin of *mulier*, woman)   449 *Answering* according to   450
were clipped about i.e. you were embraced (the passage is grammatically
incoherent)   451 *seeming* plausibility   453 *Personates* stands for   453–54
point . . . forth indicate   456 *issue* descendants

CYMBELINE   Well,
My peace we will begin. And, Caius Lucius,
Although the victor, we submit to Caesar
And to the Roman empire, promising
To pay our wonted tribute, from the which
We were dissuaded by our wicked queen,
Whom heavens in justice, both on her and hers,   463
Have laid most heavy hand.

SOOTHSAYER
The fingers of the pow'rs above do tune
The harmony of this peace. The vision   466
Which I made known to Lucius ere the stroke
Of this yet scarce-cold battle, at this instant
Is full accomplished ; for the Roman eagle,
From south to west on wing soaring aloft,
Lessened herself and in the beams o' th' sun
So vanished ; which foreshowed our princely eagle,
Th' imperial Caesar, should again unite
His favor with the radiant Cymbeline,
Which shines here in the west.

CYMBELINE   Laud we the gods,   475
And let our crooked smokes climb to their nostrils   476
From our blest altars. Publish we this peace
To all our subjects. Set we forward ; let   478
A Roman and a British ensign wave
Friendly together. So through Lud's town march,
And in the temple of great Jupiter
Our peace we'll ratify, seal it with feasts.
Set on there ! Never was a war did cease,   483
Ere bloody hands were washed, with such a peace.

                                                   Exeunt.

---

463 *Whom* on whom; *hers* i.e. Cloten   466 *vision* (cf. IV, ii 346 ff.)   475
Laud praise   476 *crooked* curling   478 *Set we forward* let us march   483
Set on there forward march

FOR THE BEST IN PAPERBACKS, LOOK FOR THE

In every corner of the world, on every subject under the sun, Penguin represents quality and variety—the very best in publishing today.

For complete information about books available from Penguin—including Puffins, Penguin Classics, and Arkana—and how to order them, write to us at the appropriate address below. Please note that for copyright reasons the selection of books varies from country to country.

In the United Kingdom: Please write to *Dept. JC, Penguin Books Ltd, FREEPOST, West Drayton, Middlesex UB7 0BR*.

If you have any difficulty in obtaining a title, please send your order with the correct money, plus ten percent for postage and packaging, to *P.O. Box No. 11, West Drayton, Middlesex UB7 0BR*

In the United States: Please write to *Consumer Sales, Penguin USA, P.O. Box 999, Dept. 17109, Bergenfield, New Jersey 07621-0120.* VISA and MasterCard holders call 1-800-253-6476 to order all Penguin titles

In Canada: Please write to *Penguin Books Canada Ltd, 10 Alcorn Avenue, Suite 300, Toronto, Ontario M4V 3B2*

In Australia: Please write to *Penguin Books Australia Ltd, P.O. Box 257, Ringwood, Victoria 3134*

In New Zealand: Please write to *Penguin Books (NZ) Ltd, Private Bag 102902, North Shore Mail Centre, Auckland 10*

In India: Please write to *Penguin Books India Pvt Ltd, 706 Eros Apartments, 56 Nehru Place, New Delhi 110 019*

In the Netherlands: Please write to *Penguin Books Netherlands bv, Postbus 3507, NL-1001 AH Amsterdam*

In Germany: Please write to *Penguin Books Deutschland GmbH, Metzlerstrasse 26, 60594 Frankfurt am Main*

In Spain: Please write to *Penguin Books S.A., Bravo Murillo 19, 1° B, 28015 Madrid*

In Italy: Please write to *Penguin Italia s.r.l., Via Felice Casati 20, I-20124 Milano*

In France: Please write to *Penguin France S.A., 17 rue Lejeune, F-31000 Toulouse*

In Japan: Please write to *Penguin Books Japan, Ishikiribashi Building, 2-5-4, Suido, Bunkyo-ku, Tokyo 112*

In Greece: Please write to *Penguin Hellas Ltd, Dimocritou 3, GR-106 71 Athens*

In South Africa: Please write to *Longman Penguin Southern Africa (Pty) Ltd, Private Bag X08, Bertsham 2013*

The Pelican Shakespeare

_____ 0-14-071430-8 **All's Well That Ends Well** Barish (ed.)

_____ 0-14-071420-0 **Antony and Cleopatra** Mack (ed.)

_____ 0-14-071417-0 **As You Like It** Sargent (ed.)

_____ 0-14-071432-4 **The Comedy of Errors** Jorgensen (ed.)

_____ 0-14-071402-2 **Coriolanus** Levin (ed.)

_____ 0-14-071428-6 **Cymbeline** Heilman (ed.)

_____ 0-14-071405-7 **Hamlet** Farnham (ed.)

_____ 0-14-071407-3 **Henry IV, Part I** Shaaber (ed.)

_____ 0-14-071408-1 **Henry IV, Part II** Chester (ed.)

_____ 0-14-071409-X **Henry V** Harbage (ed.)

_____ 0-14-071434-0 **Henry VI (Revised Edition), Part I** Bevington (ed.)

_____ 0-14-071435-9 **Henry VI (Revised Edition), Parts II and III** Bevington (ed.) Turner (ed.)

_____ 0-14-071436-7 **Henry VIII** Hoeniger (ed.)

_____ 0-14-071422-7 **Julius Caesar** Johnson (ed.)

_____ 0-14-071426-X **King John** Ribner (ed.)

_____ 0-14-071414-6 **King Lear** Harbage (ed.)

_____ 0-14-071427-8 **Love's Labor's Lost** Harbage (ed.)

_____ 0-14-071401-4 **Macbeth** Harbage (ed.)

_____ 0-14-071403-0 **Measure for Measure** Bald (ed.)

_____ 0-14-071421-9 **The Merchant of Venice** Stirling (ed.)

_____ 0-14-071424-3 **The Merry Wives of Windsor** Bowers (ed.)

The Penguin Shakespeare

The Complete Pelican
SHAKESPEARE

To fill the need for a convenient and authoritative one-volume edition, the thirty-eight books in the Pelican series have been brought together.

THE COMPLETE PELICAN SHAKESPEARE includes all the material contained in the separate volumes, together with a 50,000-word General Introduction and full bibliographies. It contains the first nineteen pages of the First Folio in reduced facsimile, five new drawings, and illustrated endpapers. 9¾ × 7³⁄₁₆ inches, 1520 pages.